THE RAPTURE BOOK

PRESENTED TO: _____

ON: _____

MESSAGE: _____

_____

_____

_____

_____

_____

_____

_____

_____

_____

_____

_____

_____

_____

PRESENTED BY: _____

"About the Time of the End,
a body of men will be raised up
who will turn their attention to the Prophecies,
and insist upon their literal interpretation,
in the midst of much clamor and opposition."

—Sir Isaac Newton

"I have been in countries where the saints are already
suffering terrible persecution. In China the Christians were
told, 'Don't worry, before the tribulation comes, you will be
translated—raptured.' Then came a terrible persecution. Mil-
lions of Christians were tortured to death. Later I heard a
bishop from China say, sadly, 'We have failed. We should have
made the people strong for persecution rather than telling
them Jesus would come first.'

"Turning to me he said, 'You still have time. Tell the peo-
ple how to be strong in times of persecution, how to stand
when the tribulation comes—to stand and not faint.'

"I feel I have a divine mandate to go and tell the people
of this world that it is possible to be strong in the Lord Jesus
Christ. We are in training for the tribulation....

"Since I have gone already through prison for Jesus sake,
and since I met that bishop from China, now every time I read
a good Bible text I think 'Hey, I can use that in the time of
tribulation.' Then I write it down and learn it by heart."

—Corrie ten Boom

THE
RAPTURE
BOOK

VICTORY IN THE END TIMES

Dr. James McKeever

THE RAPTURE BOOK

Copyright © 1987 by James M. McKeever

Printed in the United States of America
First printing June, 1987
Second printing December, 1987
Third printing October, 1988

Omega Publications
P.O. Box 4130
Medford, Oregon 97501 (U.S.A.)

ISBN #0-86694-106-1 (Softback)

TABLE OF CONTENTS

Appendices

This book is dedicated first and foremost to the glory of God and His Son, Jesus Christ.

On the human level, this book is dedicated to
all of the pastors, teachers, evangelists,
prophets and apostles that God has set
over the church today to help believers become
more like Jesus Christ,
and to every Christain who is or will become
a bondslave of Christ and have victory
during the end times of this age.

A special dedication is made to the
Omega Staff, Omega Family and Omega Team,
without whose prayers and support this book
could never have been written.

FOREWORD

By Jim Spillman

It is rare indeed for our searching eyes and hungry hearts to come upon a book that is at once forthright, persuasive and fully clothed with the word of God. Most books dealing with eschatological matters use Scripture as a minor premise and the author's opinion as the major premise. It is no wonder, then, that the syllogistic conclusion is the author's and not God's.

James McKeever not only refuses to use this strong-man approach that leads to man's opinion of God's truth, but forces the reader to hold his conclusions next to the canon of Scripture. It is common for one of his pages to have more of God's word than James' words. He, unlike many Christian authors, actually believes that God has the verbal ability to explain what He proclaims. He abides by this method of writing as well as any author I know. This gives the reader great confidence that he is viewing truth and not fiction.

The subject of this book has more of a need to be taught today to Christians than any other that I can think.

James McKeever's writing is forceful, yet gentle and humble. He holds his pen in a mailed fist, covered with a velvet glove. This book should be and, I predict, will be a best seller.

—Jim Spillman
Author, Pastor, Evangelist & Bible Scholar

I went from our Good Friday service here at noon directly to my office where I closed the door and buried my head (and heart) in the manuscript of your *Rapture Book.* I came away refreshed, renewed and shouting a glad Easter Hallelujah! This book is going to have a blessed ministry to the body of Christ, James. Our Lord is magnified from beginning to end, and when He is lifted up He draws like a magnet!...

One thing is sure, James, "Old disciples go on learning" (at least we should) and you help me in the process. I like your 3 R's. Thanks brother. We cannot know when it will all take place, but we can keep on the alert!

—Dr. F. Carlton Booth
Treasurer, World Vision
Former Professor, Fuller Theological Seminary

The Rapture Book has my unqualified recommendation. I loved it and gained many new insights through its pages.

As an attorney, it is my professional practice to read through documents for clarity and consistency. Dr. James McKeever maintains both of these throughout the entire length of this book. It's an exceptional work!

—Roger L. Minor
Attorney at Law

INTRODUCTION

Hosts of Christians around the world believe that we are living in the end of this age. This does not mean that this is the end of the world. The previous age ended when Jesus Christ came to the earth for the first time, and this age will end when Jesus Christ returns to the earth.

Most Christians are very unknowledgeable as to how the Bible says this age will end. Because of this lack of knowledge, many will perish, unnecessarily. The Bible clearly tells us about the events that will occur at the end of this age and what things we should be prepared for.

Because of a lack of knowledge, many Christians will go through the end of this age in defeat and despair. However, God has made a provision so that we can go through what lies ahead with real power and victory. In this work, I share with you the things the Lord has shown me about how we can go through the end of this age triumphantly. We can experience victory rather than defeat. We can experience jubilation rather than despair, but we need to have *both* the knowledge and the commitment to experience His protection and His power.

Just as God protected Daniel in the lion's den, and Shadrach, Meshach and Abed-nego in the fiery furnace, He is going to protect *some* Christians during the turbulent events during the end of this age. He is going to give them supernatural power beyond anything Christians have experienced up until now. Jesus Christ is raising up an end-time army, and that army will be victorious through the power of Jesus Christ and for His glory.

Unfortunately, there will be many Christian civilian casualties. This book tells you how you can become part of the victorious end-time army of Jesus Christ and go through the end of this age with victory. My prayer for you is that, as you read this work, the Lord will use it in your life to make you a victorious soldier of Jesus Christ.

Your servant in Christ,

James McKeever

ACKNOWLEDGEMENTS

In thinking of whom to acknowledge for this book, Jesus Christ instantly comes to mind. I thank Jesus for dying for me and giving me new life. I also thank the Holy Spirit for teaching me, guiding me and bringing me to a position where I want to follow Jesus Christ with all my heart, regardless of the cost.

On the human level, first and foremost, I am indebted to my wonderful wife, Jeani. She not only edited the book and provided many helpful suggestions and insights, but she actually wrote a portion of it. Her contributions were so significant that she should probably be listed as the co-author of this book. At the same time, she performed the critical functions of a writer's wife, giving me encouragement and inspiration. I praise the Lord for her. She has been the perfect wife and co-laborer, and I continually thank the Lord for her.

I also appreciate the outstanding work of Jackie Cunningham and Kay Berryman in typing the manuscript, as well as the proofreading done by Jim Andrews. In addition, I am indebted to the dear brothers of mine who read through the manuscript and gave me their constructive feedback.

I am indebted to the Christian leaders who have been bold enough to take a public stand concerning the end of this age—those who are declaring to the body of Christ that they need to know the truth and be prepared to experience some difficult days. God bless these men for their courage to take a stand opposite to the popular "party line."

I also appreciate the prayers and the encouragement of a whole host of people, especially the Omega Family and the Omega Team and our staff here at Omega Ministries headquarters. God honors and answers the prayers of His people. We all prayed that a book would be produced that would help the body of Christ to know the truth about the end of this age and a book that would glorify Jesus Christ in every way. I believe that God has answered these prayers, and, therefore, we dedicate this book to the glory of Jesus Christ and God the Father.

James McKeever

PREFACE

By Jeani McKeever

Some of the truths uncovered in this book are hard-hitting and may require change and growth, as you allow the Holy Spirit to expand your thinking. You will appreciate, as I do, the inclusion of Scripture references written out in full, so you can read them for yourself. This way, you can make up your own mind as to what the Scriptures are saying, and you can draw your own conclusions as to the validity of the author's interpretation.

You may well find that this book answers many questions you have had about end-time events, and perhaps it will challenge you in some new areas of thinking. That's good. If it forces you back to seek God's face and His truth as it is revealed in the Scriptures, then we have provided a worthy service.

This one thing I do know about James—he is a man of integrity, and his motivation in writing this book is to help people by sharing what insights God has given to him. I believe that you will come to agree with me that this book is a needful challenge to the church to find out *why* we believe *what* we believe.

May God greatly bless and enrich you through the reading of these pages.

1

WE ALL WANT VICTORY

As we all watched the 16 days of the 1984 Olympics, our hearts pulled for the athletes and cheered them as they won their events. Everyone likes a champion; everyone likes a winner.

God wants you to be a winner and you can be a winner and experience the joy of victory. It does not matter your occupation, your age or your status in life. God wants you to be a winner and to experience victory.

We can see in the Old Testament many victorious heros. We think of Joshua marching around Jericho with the walls falling down and all the troops rushing forward for a day of victory and rejoicing. Our thoughts turn to Elijah calling down fire from heaven to consume the offering, the altar and the water in the trench around, thus putting to total defeat the prophets of Baal.

Other victories in the Old Testament were achieved as people went through difficult times. There was Daniel going through the lion's den. However, he went through it with God's divine protection and, through the power of God, had a tremendous victory. We all remember the three young Hebrew men, Shadrach, Meshach, and Abed-nego, who went through the fiery furnace, but again with God's divine protection, and had a real day of victory and triumph.

In Jesus' day, many had true victories. As the disciples went out two by two and healed the sick and cast out demons, they came back rejoicing over the victory that they had had through the power and authority of Jesus Christ. As he traveled about converting the Gentile world, Paul had victory after victory and triumph after triumph.

The same thing is true today. Christians everywhere are winning victories. They are winning victories in the financial world, in the political world, in the athletic world and on every side. God wants you to join in this triumphal parade headed by Jesus Christ and experience the power and victory that is available to you.

As this age ends, we are especially going to want to have victory during those days. We want to war against Satan and evil in the world and to come through triumphant. We want to overcome them. As strange and sometimes frightening things begin to happen at the end of this age, we are going to want to be in a victorious position of being able to help others and comfort others and certainly not come away defeated. But before we proceed in thinking about victory during the end of this age, we need to look at what ages actually are and if the age we are living in is drawing to a close.

AGES IN THE BIBLE

Jesus Himself did a great deal of teaching about the end of this age and He did it for a reason, and it is in the Bible for a reason. He wants us to read about it and understand it. Very possibly, He gave some of those teachings specifically for this generation, and we cannot afford to ignore them.

Approximately one-third of the Bible is prophecy. Those who ignore prophecy are rejecting one-third of what the Lord wants them to know. Satan will try to keep a Christian away from that one-third of the Bible. God knew that, and perhaps that is why He promised a blessing to those who would read and heed Revelation (Revelation 1:3). God wants *YOU* to understand the events of the end times of this age.

Let me first state that I am not a dispensationalist, although many dear brothers of mine in Jesus Christ are of that persuasion. (If you are not familiar with the dispensational theory taught by Dallas Theological Seminary, these three paragraphs will not be relevant to you.) In an attempt to give us a framework onto which to hang the teachings of the Bible, the dispensationalists have done us a great deal of good; but, unfortunately, there has been some harm with it. For example, they tell us that the Sermon on the Mount, and basically Jesus' teachings prior to the cross, were for the Jewish people of that day and were not intended to be for Christians. Yet Jesus Himself commands us:

> **19** **"Go therefore and make disciples of all the nations, baptizing them in the name of the Father and the Son and the Holy Spirit,**
> **20** **teaching them to observe all that I commanded you; and lo, I am with you always, even to the end of the age."**
>
> **—Matthew 28**

Here we see that Jesus commanded us to teach people to observe *all* that He commanded us (in the four Gospels). Thus, I believe Jesus Himself placed the writings of the Gospels into the age in which we live.

Even though I am not a dispensationalist, I do recognize that the Bible, and Jesus Himself, divided history into "ages." In fact, in verse 20 of Matthew 28 that we just read, Jesus told the disciples that He would be with them, even to the end of this age. As we will see, that is the end of the age in which we are now living.

We might look at a few of the Scriptures wherein the Bible teaches that there are various "ages." First we see that the Bible teaches that there were ages prior to the one in which we are living:

> **9** **and to bring to light what is the administration of the mystery which for ages has been hidden in God, who created all things;...**
>
> **—Ephesians 3**

> **26** ***that is,*** **the mystery which has been hidden from the *past* ages and generations; but has now been manifested to His saints,...**
>
> **—Colossians 1**

25   Now to Him who is able to establish you according to my gospel and the preaching of Jesus Christ, according to the revelation of the mystery which has been kept secret for long ages past, . . .

—Romans 16

The Bible also clearly teaches us that there will be at least two ages to come after the one in which we are presently living. Thus, we can conclude that planet earth is going to be around for awhile, so we are not talking about the end of the world. Here we see that the Bible says there will be future ages:

30   but that he shall receive a hundred times as much now in the present age, houses and brothers and sisters and mothers and children and farms, along with persecutions; and in the age to come, eternal life.

—Mark 10

7   in order that in the ages to come He might show the surpassing riches of His grace in kindness toward us in Christ Jesus.

—Ephesians 2

Now that we have seen that there were ages in the past and there are ages to come, let us see if we can clear up some confusion about our present age and how it will end. We will frequently be coming back to Matthew 24 during this book, but let us begin by looking at the basic question that the disciples asked Jesus that day on the Mount of Olives:

3   And as He was sitting on the Mount of Olives, the disciples came to Him privately, saying, "Tell us, when will these things be, and what *will be* the sign of Your coming, and of the end of the age?"

—Matthew 24

In this verse we see the disciples asking Jesus to tell them clearly what it will be like at the end of this age—that is, the age containing the return of the Lord. Therefore, it is obvious that the age that we are living in, the age that contains Jesus' coming, had already started as Jesus was sitting there on the Mount of Olives with His disciples. The disciples did not ask how the "next" age would end. Rather, they asked how the present age would end, the age containing His Second Coming, the age we are living in at present.

We do not know when this current age began. It could have begun at Jesus' conception, at His birth, at His circumcision when He was eight days old, when He was twelve years old in the temple, or at His baptism by John when He began His public ministry. Whenever it began, it is very clear that, as Jesus was sitting here on the Mount of Olives, the age that you and I are living in had already started, the age that contains His Second Coming. Thus, in the teachings of Christ, when He teaches about the present age, He is teaching about the age that you and I are living in. When he talks about the "end of the age" (the end times), He is talking about the end of this very age that you and I are living in. He taught us the following:

39   and the enemy who sowed them is the devil, and the harvest is the end of the age; and the reapers are angels.
40   "Therefore just as the tares are gathered up and burned with fire, so shall it be at the end of the age...."
49   "So it will be at the end of the age; the angels shall come forth, and take out the wicked from among the righteous,...

—Matthew 13

20   teaching them to observe all that I commanded you; and lo, I am with you always, even to the end of the age."

—Matthew 28

8   "And his master praised the unrighteous steward because he had acted shrewdly; for the sons of this age are more shrewd in relation to their own kind than the sons of light...."

—Luke 16

29   And He said to them, "Truly I say to you, there is no one who has left house or wife or brothers or parents or children, for the sake of the kingdom of God,

**30   who shall not receive many times as much at this
time and in the age to come, eternal life."**

—Luke 18

From the verses above, you can see that Jesus taught that the age that we are living in will end and certain things are going to happen during the end of this age, such as His sending out the angels to do the reaping. He also taught that there will be another age, after the end of the one in which we are now living.

Many people have come up with various constructions for past ages, and that is not a subject that I feel the Lord wants me to address here. However, we know that one giant age ended when God intervened on planet earth through the Ten Commandments and then the rules changed about how one rightly related to God. The next giant age ended when God once again intervened on planet earth and sent His Son, Jesus Christ. Once again the rules changed about how one rightly relates to God. Those were very lucky people who saw that change of the ages when Christ lived here on the earth. It was not the end of the world; it was simply that one age ended and another began.

The Bible, and especially Jesus Himself, has a great deal to say about how this age is going to end. Many Christian leaders, and really the body of Christ at large all around the world, have a feeling that we are the generation that is going to see the end times of this age and Jesus Christ return to the earth. If this is true, and especially if you personally feel that way, then this book is very important for you, to help you understand what is coming and be prepared for it.

THE TIME OF CREATION
VERSUS THE TIME OF RESTORATION

In Chapter 11, we will be looking in detail at the question, "Are we living in the end times?", examining prophecies and world events to see if the prophecies concerning the end of this age are being fulfilled today.

However, right now we would like to give just one thought that might indicate that the age we are living in is about to wrap up.

Evidently, God has a different measurement of time than we do. In Genesis 1, we find that God did something on the first day, then on the second day, and then on the third day. However, the sun and the moon were not created until the *fourth day* of creation. Since we measure our days by a rotation of the earth in relationship to the sun, there must have been some other way to measure days during the first three days of creation.

God must have His own clock and it evidently runs at a different pace than ours.

In two places the Scriptures say that one thousand of our years is like one of God's days.

> **4   For a thousand years in Thy sight**
> **Are like yesterday when it passes by,**
> **Or *as* a watch in the night.**
> **   —Psalm 90**

> **8   But do not let this one *fact* escape your notice,**
> **beloved, that with the Lord one day is as a thousand**
> **years, and a thousand years as one day.**
> **   —2 Peter 3**

If a thousand of our years is equal to one day in God's eyes, then the six days of creation in Genesis could easily equate to six thousand years. The seventh day, when God rested, we could equate to one thousand years of rest.

It is interesting to note that from the fall of Adam to the call of Abraham was approximately two thousand years. Then from the call of Abraham to the first coming of Jesus Christ was approximately two thousand years. If it is approximately two thousand years from the first coming of Jesus to His Second Coming, that would make a total of six thousand years (six of God's days) of restoration.

The Bible tells us that after Jesus comes back, He will rule and reign here on the earth for a thousand years, and the earth will be restored and will be at rest. Thus, you have six of God's "days" to restore what Adam messed up and, after that, one of God's "days" of rest while Jesus Christ rules and reigns here.

The comparison of the six "days" of creation followed by a day of rest, and the six "days" of restoration followed by a day of rest is shown in Figure 1.1.

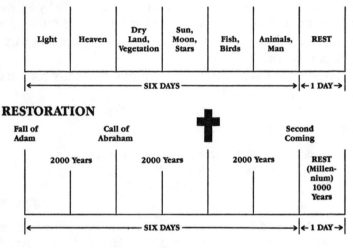

Figure 1.1

We are not saying that Jesus will come back at the year 2000. We are saying if this parallel continues to hold, it is possible that Jesus could come back around the year 2000, plus or minus thirty years. It is certainly a parallel worth considering. If we are possibly living in the times when the end of this age will wrap up, then we need to be concerned about what the Bible actually says about this. We need to know what things will be happening during the end of this age, according to the Bible. We will have more to say about this later, but for now let us assume that we are likely living in the end times of this age, and that, therefore, you want to know more about it, since it concerns you.

MY PRAYER FOR YOU

As you read this book, my prayer for you is that the Holy Spirit will teach you directly from the Scriptures. Do not take my word for anything, but go to the Scriptures, review these passages, and ask God what His truth is and He *will* reveal it to you.

We may get into some areas that are new concepts for you. Simply because something is new does not mean it is not God's truth. Jesus brought many new concepts in His teachings, and yet they were truth. Unfortunately, the Pharisees rejected His teachings, without really hearing them, thinking about them and praying about them. May the Lord give you an open mind to prayerfully examine the things that we will be sharing together.

I only want to glorify Jesus Christ and to present His truth. If there is anything in this book that is not His perfect truth, I pray that the Holy Spirit will eradicate it from your mind and memory. Conversely, I pray that the Holy Spirit will burn deep into your heart the things in this book that are His truth.

I do pray that God's richest blessings will be on you, as together we look at how this age is going to end and the next one begin.

2

THE TIME OF BIRTH PANGS THAT PRECEDES THE GREAT TRIBULATION

Evidently Jesus had taught the disciples much about this age ending and about His return. Right towards the end of His ministry, they came to Him and asked Him to tell them what it was going to be like at the end of the age. As we read in the last chapter, this question is recorded in Matthew 24:

3   And as He was sitting on the Mount of Olives, the disciples came to Him privately, saying, "Tell us, when will these things be, and what will be the sign of Your coming, and of the end of the age?"

The *King James Version* incorrectly translates the last part of this sentence as "the end of the world." The Greek word for "world" is "cosmos"; the Greek word for "age" is "aion." The Greek word used here is "aion," so it should be correctly translated "the end of the age." The disciples were asking what things would be like at the end of the age, and the age they were talking about was obviously the one that contained the Second Coming of Jesus Christ. As we have seen, that is also the age that we are living in right now.

As the disciples asked this straightforward, no-nonsense question of Jesus, I believe He gave them a straightforward, no-nonsense, chronological answer as to what the end of this age would be like and what would be occurring right before He came back.

In speaking around the world, I often ask Christian audiences to hold up their hand if they think we are likely the generation that will see Jesus return. Usually almost every hand goes up. Then I share with them that, if this is the case, they should be vitally interested in Jesus' answer to the disciples' question of what it would be like at the end of this age, because, if they held up their hand, they are also saying that they are likely going to experience the things that Jesus said would happen just prior to His return.

Do you think we are the generation that will likely see Jesus return? If your answer is "yes," you too should be very interested in what the Bible says will happen during the end times of this age, because you very likely will experience it.

Before I comment further, I would like you to read the first part of Jesus' answer to that question from the disciples. I would ask you to read it over carefully, maybe even read it twice before proceeding.

4   And Jesus answered and said to them, "See to it that no one misleads you.

5   "For many will come in My name, saying, 'I am the Christ,' and will mislead many.

6   "And you will be hearing of wars and rumors of wars; see that you are not frightened, for *those things* must take place, but *that* is not yet the end.

7   "For nation will rise against nation, and kingdom against kingdom, and in various places there will be famine and earthquakes.

8   "But all these things are *merely* the beginning of birth pangs.

10   "And at that time many will fall away and will deliver up one another and hate one another.

11   "And many false prophets will arise, and will mislead many.

12   "And because lawlessness is increased, most people's love will grow cold.

13   "But the one who endures to the end, he shall be saved.

14   "And this gospel of the kingdom shall be preached in the whole world for a witness to all the nations, and then the end shall come.

15   "Therefore when you see the ABOMINATION OF DESOLATION which was spoken of through Daniel the

prophet, standing in the holy place (let the reader understand),

16   then let those who are in Judea flee to the mountains;

17   let him who is on the housetop not go down to get the things out that are in his house;

18   and let him who is in the field not turn back to get his cloak.

19   "But woe to those who are with child and to those who nurse babes in those days!

20   "But pray that your flight may not be in the winter, or on a Sabbath;

21   for then there will be a great tribulation, such as has not occurred since the beginning of the world until now, nor ever shall...."

—Matthew 24

I trust that you have now prayerfully read the preceding passage of Scripture. If you have not, please do read it carefully before proceeding. Having read that portion of Matthew 24, I can now ask you this: when does the great tribulation start? I am sure you answered correctly that it begins in verse 21. (It is described in detail in verses 22-28.)

Many Christians have the idea that life is going to be beautiful and wonderful and then all of a sudden the bottom will drop out and the great tribulation will start. Is that what Jesus Christ taught? I'm certain that you would answer "definitely not." He taught that there would be a period of time preceding the great tribulation, which He labeled the "time of birth pangs." The *King James Version* calls it the "time of sorrows." The time of birth pangs or the time of sorrows were terms used in New Testament times for a woman in labor about to give birth to a child. What Jesus is saying is that there is going to be a time, preceding the great tribulation, wherein the earth is going to go through something equivalent to what a woman in labor experiences.

When labor pains start, they are mild and fairly far apart and, as labor progresses, the contractions get more and more intense and closer and closer together. I believe that Jesus did not accidentally choose that illustration for what is going to happen upon the earth. I am sure He knew that the traumas coming upon the earth would be mild and far apart at the beginning, and they would intensify and come more frequently as the "time of birth pangs" proceeded. So the time of birth pangs is a time preceding the great tribulation, during which conditions on the earth are going to increasingly worsen.

Some people would call the "time of birth pangs" the first half of the tribulation, and the "great tribulation" the second half of the tribulation. I can find no scriptural evidence for that concept. You certainly cannot find it based on Daniel's seventy weeks. We are far safer if we will stay with the terminology that Jesus Himself used. He said there would be a "time of birth pangs" that would precede the "great tribulation." If Jesus used those terms for those two periods of time, that is good enough for me, and that is the terminology that we will use in this book. There is no evidence that this "time of birth pangs" is ever called the tribulation, so let's lay aside man's terms and ideas and stick with what the Master said.

There are some who might try to teach that this "time of birth pangs" was accomplished in 70 A.D. when the Roman General Titus Vespasian destroyed Jerusalem. However, that does not fit. The question that Jesus was answering was what it would be like at the end of this current age, the age that contained His return. He certainly would not describe events that were going to occur in 70 A.D. in telling how this age would end. So, we see that the "time of birth pangs" is something that will occur in the end times of this age.

Even if you believe that a rapture is going to occur before the great tribulation, we are all going to go through this time of birth pangs. If the rapture indeed happens before the great tribulation, then we would have to splice it in between verses 20 and 21 of Matthew 24. However, every one of us is going to go through this time of birth pangs, if indeed we are living in the end of this age, as the Holy Spirit seems to be showing us that we are. If you believe that you are probably going to see Jesus return, then you also believe that you are going to experience this time of birth pangs, which precedes the great tribulation.

EVENTS DURING THE TIME OF BIRTH PANGS

As we carefully read in Matthew 24 what Jesus said would happen during the time of birth pangs, we see that there are nine major events that will occur. These are:

1. War (verses 6 and 7)
2. Spiritual (kingdom) war (verse 7)
3. Famines (verse 7)
4. Earthquakes (verse 7)
5. Persecution of Christians (verse 9)
6. Christians will be misled by false prophets (verse 11)
7. Lawlessness will increase (verse 12)
8. The gospel will be preached to the whole world (verse 14)
9. The abomination of desolation will appear (verse 15)

We will discuss each of these nine things in more detail later in this chapter.

In his second letter to Timothy, Paul also seemed to be talking about this time of birth pangs, from another aspect, when he described what was going to happen in the last days of this age:

1   But realize this, that in the last days difficult times will come.

2   For men will be lovers of self, lovers of money, boastful, arrogant, revilers, disobedient to parents, ungrateful, unholy,

3   unloving, irreconcilable, malicious gossips, without self-control, brutal, haters of good,

4   treacherous, reckless, conceited, lovers of pleasure rather than lovers of God;

5   holding to a form of godliness, although they have denied its power; and avoid such men as these.

6   For among them are those who enter into households and captivate weak women weighed down with sins, led on by various impulses,

7   always learning and never able to come to the knowledge of the truth.

—2 Timothy 3

Nowhere in the Bible can I find any clue as to how long this time of birth pangs will last. However, in reading the various events in it, it seems as though it would have to occur over a number of years.

Looking at the descriptions of the time of birth pangs given to us by Christ and Paul, one would begin to wonder if perhaps we are not already in the beginning stages of this time of birth pangs. Certainly lawlessness has increased; many people have a form of godliness but deny the power; there are famines many places on the earth; we seem to continually have a war someplace on the globe; and, in many countries today, persecution is coming against Christians.

If someone were to ask me point-blank if I thought we were in the time of birth pangs, I would have to answer honestly, "I don't know." However, it is certainly possible that we are.

In some ways, it doesn't matter whether or not we are in the time of birth pangs. The significant thing is that if we are the generation that is going to see Christ return to the earth, then we definitely will go through the time of birth pangs. Since it comprises events that in all likelihood you and I will experience, we need to look at those events in more detail. Before we do, we should see how the time of birth pangs—as described by Christ in Matthew 24—relates to the book of Revelation.

THE SEALS AND THE BIRTH PANGS

Revelation 6 describes six seals. When each of these seals is opened and the scroll is rolled back to the next seal, the events written in that portion of the scroll then occur on the earth.

I believe that the first five seals also describe the time of birth pangs that Christ delineates in Matthew 24, because almost the identical events occur in an almost identical sequence. Thus, I believe that we can read about the first five seals to find out more about the time of birth pangs.

Let us now look at each of the nine events that will occur during the time of birth pangs.

1.   World War

As we read in Matthew 24, Christ said that one of the things that was going to happen at the end of the age was war:

> **6   "And you will be hearing of wars and rumors of wars; see that you are not frightened, for those things must take place, but that is not yet the end.**
> **7   "For nation will rise against nation, and kingdom against kingdom, and in various places there will be famines and earthquakes...."**
> **—Matthew 24**

All that Christ says about war in Matthew 24 is that there are going to be wars and rumors of wars. You might legitimately ask why I think that this is going to be a world war. For the answer to that, let's turn to Revelation 6:

> **3   And when he broke the second seal, I heard the second living creature saying, "Come."**
> **4   And another, a red horse, went out; and to him who sat on it, it was granted to take peace from the earth, and that men should slay one another; and a great sword was given to him.**

In verse 4, we see that when this seal is opened, peace is going to be taken from the entire earth. Not even World War I or World War II took peace from the entire earth; South America was not really involved in those wars.

However, in the war that is coming during the time of birth pangs, the Bible says that peace will be taken from the *entire earth*. Thus, we can legitimately call it a world war. In fact, it is probably going to be the first real world war. Verse 4 also says that peace is going to be taken from the earth "with a great sword," or we could legitimately say with "a great weapon." There may be other things that could happen that would fulfill this prophecy, but a nuclear war certainly would fulfill it. If there were radioactive fallout circling the globe, men in every nation would be dying and peace would be taken from the earth, and certainly a nuclear bomb would be classified as "a great weapon."

This is why I believe that during the time of birth pangs we will definitely have a world war, and it will most likely be nuclear in nature. If indeed you believe that you will see Jesus return, then there is a great likelihood that you will experience this nuclear war. In my book, *Christians Will Go Through The Tribulation—And How To Prepare For It,* I give a great deal of information on how you can survive a nuclear war in order to be alive when it is over to be able to help people and to witness to them. I am convinced that God wants Christians to live through this war. There is much that He wants us to do on the other side. Opportunities for His kingdom will be great during such a time.

Concerning the dead after this war, it will not be the birds eating the dead, as is described in Revelation 19:17-18. That occurs after the battle of Armageddon, when Christ returns in power and glory. It is not the time that requires seven months to bury the dead, as described in Ezekiel 39:12 (following the Gog-Magog war, which occurs at the end of the millennium, according to Revelation 20:7-10). As far as I can find in the Scriptures, we do not know how the dead from this war will be removed. However, remember, with so many dead, it is likely that almost every family will have lost someone. Those who are sorrowing will need comforting and will need to hear about our Savior, Jesus Christ. Guess who God wants to carry that message?

2. Spiritual War

We also read about spiritual war in Matthew 24:

7 "For nation will rise against nation, and kingdom against kingdom,..."

When this verse says "nation will rise against nation," I believe it speaks of political entities, as we know them today. However, when it says "kingdom against kingdom," I believe it is talking about the kingdom of Christ versus the kingdom of Satan. Thus, we see that one of the significant occurrences during the time of birth pangs is a massive spiritual war.

At a world convention of the Full Gospel Businessmen's Fellowship International, I heard Pat Robertson (founder of Christian Broadcasting Network) minister on Satan as the accuser of the brothers. He pointed out that right now Satan not only has access to the earth, but his primary place is standing before the throne of God accusing the brothers night and day. I would certainly agree that that is where Satan is today.

What this means, though, is that the war in heaven—wherein Satan is kicked out of heaven with a third of the angels (and will no longer have access to the throne of God)—is yet in the future. In my book, *You Can Overcome*, I delve into passages which could be construed to indicate that the war in heaven has already occurred, but upon closer examination, one discovers that they do not necessarily teach this. The war in heaven, wherein Satan and one-third of the angels are kicked out, is described in Revelation 12. There it tells us that when the war occurs, Satan will only have a short time left (three and a half years, possibly?). If the war occurred thousands of years ago, the criterion of "only a short time" would not apply.

7   And there was war in heaven, Michael and his angels waging war with the dragon. And the dragon and his angels waged war,

8   and they were not strong enough, and there was no longer a place found for them in heaven.

9   And the great dragon was thrown down, the serpent of old who is called the devil and Satan, who deceived the whole world; he was thrown down to the earth, and his angels were thrown down with him.

10   And I heard a loud voice in heaven, saying,

"Now the salvation, and the power, and the kingdom of our god and the authority of His Christ have come,

for the accuser of our brethren has been thrown down, who accuses them before our God day and night.

11   "And they overcame him because of the blood of the Lamb and because of the word of their testimony, and they did not love their life even to death.

12   "For this reason, rejoice, O heavens and you who dwell in them. Woe to the earth and the sea, because the devil has come down to you, having great wrath, knowing that he has only a short time."

—Revelation 12

Through the centuries, God has raised up overcomers. However, today He seems to be raising up a whole army of overcomers. I asked the Lord why He was raising up such an army. This is when He showed me from the Scriptures that this war in heaven had not yet occurred.

I sensed in my spirit that He was raising up an overcomer army so that when Satan loses the war in heaven and hits the earth, with a third of the angels who will fall with him, this army of Christ's will come against Satan and will overcome him. Praise God!

Verse 11 of Revelation 12 tells us how we will overcome Satan:

1. By the blood of the Lamb
2. By the word of our testimony
3. We do not love our life even unto death

God wants you to be part of that overcomer army that will defeat Satan during the time of birth pangs. The book, *You Can Overcome,* delves into this in more detail and can help you learn to be an effective soldier and overcomer for God.

The book of Revelation is definitely not chronological, as we will see before this book is over. This is why it is not violating scriptural interpretation to take an event in Revelation 12 and to apply it to the time of birth pangs. This is discussed in detail in my book, *Now You Can Understand The Book Of Revelation.* No significant Bible scholar that I have read considers the book of Revelation to be a purely chronological book.

So we see that one of the major events during the time of birth pangs (possibly very near to the beginning of the great tribulation) is going to be a spiritual war. We have had spiritual battles up until now, but there is a major spiritual war coming, in which the kingdom of Christ is going to come against the kingdom of Satan and defeat it. I trust and pray that you will be part of Christ's overcomer army (not all Christians are part of that army) that will overcome Satan in this coming spiritual war.

3.   Famines

Jesus also said that famines would occur at the end of this age, during the time of birth pangs:

> **7   "For nation will rise against nation, and kingdom against kingdom, and in various places there will be famines and earthquakes...."**
>
> **—Matthew 24**

You will notice that this says there are going to be famines in various places. I do not believe that this means that one nation will be starving while another will have plenty of food. Rather, I believe it means that in various places across the world there will be very little, if any, food produced at all. With our worldwide transportation system, the prices of wheat, corn, and cattle are all worldwide prices. Thus, when the famine hits, it will affect the entire globe.

I believe that the magnitude of this famine is spelled out in detail in the third seal:

> **5   And when He broke the third seal, I heard the third living creature saying, "Come." And I looked, and behold, a black horse; and he who sat on it had a pair of scales in his hand.**
>
> **6   And I heard as it were a voice in the center of the four living creatures saying, "A quart of wheat for a**

denarius, and three quarts of barley for a denarius; and do not harm the oil and the wine."

—**Revelation 6**

If you read the footnotes in your Bible, you will see that a denarius is equivalent to one day's wage for the average working man. So what verse 6 tells us is that the famine is going to be so bad that it will take one day's wage to buy a quart of wheat.

How long do you think a quart of wheat would feed a family of four? Since my wife, Jeani, grinds wheat and makes our own bread, we have some idea of how long that much wheat would last. A quart of wheat, ground into flour for bread or eaten as cooked cereal, would feed a family of four for roughly one day.

What this says is that the famine will be so bad that 100 percent of the average man's wage will go to buy food. It will take one day's wage to buy one day's worth of food. This means that there will be nothing left over for rent, gasoline, clothes, or anything else. This is not *my* idea, nor the ravings of a prophet of doom; this is simply what the Bible says is going to occur at the end of this age.

The economic and social implications are absolutely incredible. If there is not money left over for anything except food, and people cannot make the payments on the loans on their homes, the banking system will collapse. If there is nothing left over to buy gasoline, there goes the automobile industry. Thus, this famine, with tentacles reaching out like an octopus, will crush the entire economies of nations. This means that inflation will go beyond a runaway condition and be totally out of control.

If we indeed see Jesus return to the earth, then we will be going through this famine, and the economic chaos it will bring, that Jesus said would happen during the time of birth pangs.

4. Earthquakes

Jesus said that there were going to be earthquakes in various places during the time of birth pangs:

> **7 "...and in various places there will be famines and earthquakes.**
> **8 "But all these things are merely the beginning of birth pangs...."**
>
> **—Matthew 24**

There will be a "great earthquake" or, as I like to call it, an "earth upheaval" after the time of birth pangs is over. However, during the time of birth pangs, there is evidently going to be an increased incidence of earthquakes and an increase in their intensity, since this is one of the signs that the Lord told us to look for.

5. Persecution of Christians

In his book, *'till Armageddon,* Billy Graham pointed out that Christians need to get ready to suffer in general and, specifically, to suffer persecution, from now until the battle of Armageddon. (The battle of Armageddon, of course, occurs at the end of the great tribulation.) Many other writers, such as Dave Wilkerson, have also warned Christians to get ready for persecution. These writers are right on target with what Christ had to say:

> **9 "Then they will deliver you to tribulation, and will kill you, and you will be hated by all nations on account of My name.**
> **10 "And at that time many will fall away and will deliver up one another and hate one another...."**
>
> **—Matthew 24**

We see here that many Christians will be killed because they cling to the name of Jesus. The sad thing is that many Christians will fall away and many will become traitors and will deliver up other followers of Jesus Christ to the authorities (verse 10). It also says that these "Christians" who turn in the true, solid believers will actually hate them. Thus, we see the persecution coming out of "Christendom," as well as from non-Christian sources.

It was this way in the time of Jesus and in the early centuries of Christianity. In fact, it was the religious leaders who ultimately crucified Jesus.

In talking to missionaries returning from places where communist governments have come in or dictators have taken over and persecution has begun, they say that their greatest problem was traitors within the church. For example, one of these traitors that looks like a sheep, but is really a wolf, turns in the name of the pastor to the authorities. The pastor is then arrested and disappears. God raises up a new leader. However, the traitor strikes again and the authorities arrest the new leader.

When this persecution comes, and when it comes from those we thought were our dear Christian brothers, we should not be surprised, because Jesus forewarned us that it was coming.

The fifth seal in Revelation 6 gives us some more details about those who are going to be martyred for the sake of Jesus Christ:

> **9   And when He broke the fifth seal, I saw underneath the altar the souls of those who had been slain because of the word of God, and because of the testimony which they had maintained;**
>
> **10   and they cried out with a loud voice, saying, "How long, O Lord, holy and true, wilt Thou refrain from judging and avenging our blood on those who dwell on the earth?"**
>
> **11   And there was given to each of them a white robe; and they were told that they should rest for a little while longer, until the number of their fellow servants and their brethren who were to be killed even as they had been, should be completed also.**
>
> **—Revelation 6**

We would like to think that if we were martyred for Jesus, God would immediately repay the bad people who martyred us. This would probably apply even more so if someone were to kill our children. We would want to take vengeance on that person or to have God immediately take vengeance on him. However, as you read those three verses out of Revelation 6, you see that God is going to wait before judging and avenging the deaths of the martyrs.

Persecution is coming, even to America, and we need to be spiritually ready for it and to be sure that our families and our churches are spiritually ready for it. One of the things that would be very beneficial would be to know for sure, in your home Bible study group (or "cell" meeting, or whatever they are called in your church), who is truly committed to Jesus Christ and to the other Christians there—to know who would be willing to lay down his life rather than betray his brothers and sisters in Jesus. Now is the time to develop a covenant commitment with others who are willing to be martyred for Jesus Christ.

6.   Some Christians
Will Be Misled by False Prophets

Many are going to be misled during the time of birth pangs:

> **11   "And many false prophets will arise, and will mislead many...."**
>
> **—Matthew 24**

The false prophets will look like regular Christian teachers. One of their characteristics is that they will tell people what they want to hear. This is another way of saying they will "tickle their ears." This is described in Paul's second letter to Timothy:

> **3   For the time will come when they will not endure sound doctrine by wanting to have their ears tickled, they will accumulate for themselves teachers in accordance to their own desires;**
> **4   and will turn away their ears from the truth, and will turn aside to myths.**
>
> **—2 Timothy 4**

People would like to hear that everything is going to be wonderful, that they are not going to have to endure any hardships, that they won't have to suffer, and that life is getting better and better. They also love to hear that when Jesus comes they will instantly be made perfect, so they don't have to press to become holy here on the earth. The list of what people want to hear could go on and on. Christians who flock after teachers who propagate such teachings will be misled. Jesus warned us, in Matthew 24, that we would see many being misled during the time of birth pangs.

7.   Lawlessness Will Increase

People's regard for the law and for authority continues to diminish. Jesus said that during the time of birth pangs, this attitude would increase:

12   "And because lawlessness is increased, most people's love will grow cold...."
—Matthew 24

We do not know if the lawlessness to which Jesus was referring pertains to the laws of one's nation or the laws of God. It really doesn't matter because, as I travel around the world today, I see men respecting neither God's laws nor the laws of their nation.

Even many Christians delight in cheating on their taxes, exceeding the 55-miles-per-hour speed limit and, in general, breaking the law. This disregard for the law and authority is likely to increase to the point that we could see a real breakdown of law and order in our cities.

8.   The Gospel Will Be Preached
To the Whole World

Now we get to one of the most exciting events that is going to happen during the time of birth pangs. Jesus also told us about this in Matthew 24:

14 "And this gospel of the kingdom shall be preached in the whole world for a witness to all the nations, and then the end shall come...."

Before the end of the age comes, the gospel of the kingdom will be preached to the whole world. Incidently, it does not say, "the gospel of salvation." There is more to the gospel than just getting people to pray a little prayer for God's goodies and salvation. The kingdom of God is the form of government in which God is the sole ruler. Thus, the message of God's rulership in the individual's heart and life must be taken to all nations before the end comes.

If there is one subject that is the umbrella which covers the entire Bible and the span of the centuries, it is the kingdom of God. Christians will spend eternity in the kingdom of God, and yet most people understand so little about it.

But for now, the important point is that the gospel of the kingdom will go out to all nations before this age ends, and I am excited to be part of that outreach and trust that you will be too.

Every Christian should be deeply concerned about the gospel going to the whole world. We should all be praying for the salvation of souls and for the missionaries and ministries around the world, as well as financially contributing to those who are helping to take the gospel to the whole earth. There is a great revival coming during this time of birth pangs, and you and I can be part of that!

In addition to supporting and being concerned about those people who do not know Jesus as King and Savior in other parts of the world, you should also be concerned about your own community. Be praying that God would lead you to people near you with whom you can share the good news about Jesus Christ, the King, and His transforming power.

I believe the gospel being taken to all the world is depicted by the white horse in Revelation 6:

> **1** And I saw when the Lamb broke one of the seven seals, and I heard one of the four living creatures saying as with a voice of thunder, "Come."
> **2** And I looked, and behold, a white horse, and he who sat on it had a bow; and a crown was given to him; and he went out conquering, and to conquer.

There are some who think that this white horse is "the Antichrist," but never in the Bible is evil depicted as white. I believe this is Christians going out conquering in the name of Christ and winning into His kingdom those who will listen to the gospel and receive Christ as their Savior and Lord.

There is another white horse that appears later in the book of Revelation (Revelation 19:11-16). Christ is going to ride upon it as He returns to the earth. I believe our spreading the gospel of the kingdom to all the world is depicted this way to encourage us as we go forth in the spiritual war, conquering in the name of Christ.

9. The Abomination of Desolation

One of the events that Christ says will occur during the time of birth pangs is the abomination of desolation spoken of by Daniel the prophet:

> **15** "Therefore when you see the ABOMINATION OF DESOLATION which was spoken of through Daniel the prophet, standing in the holy place (let the reader understand),
> **16** then let those who are in Judea flee to the mountains;
> **17** let him who is on the housetop not go down to get the things out that are in his house;
> **18** and let him who is in the field not turn back to get his cloak...."
>
> **—Matthew 24**

I believe this abomination of desolation is the one discussed in Daniel 12 and possibly Daniel 11:

9 And he said, "Go your way, Daniel, for these words are concealed and sealed up until the end time.

10 "Many will be purged, purified and refined; but the wicked will act wickedly, and none of the wicked will understand, but those who have insight will understand.

11 "And from the time that the regular sacrifice is abolished, and the abomination of desolation is set up, there will be 1,290 days.

—Daniel 12

31 "And forces from him will arise, desecrate the sanctuary fortress, and do away with the regular sacrifice. And they will set up the abomination of desolation.

32 "And by smooth words he will turn to godlessness those who act wickedly toward the covenant, but the people who know their God will display strength and take action.

33 "And those who have insight among the people will give understanding to the many; yet they will fall by sword and by flame, by captivity and by plunder, for many days.

34 "Now when they fall they will be granted a little help, and many will join with them in hypocrisy.

35 "And some of those who have insight will fall, in order to refine, purge, and make them pure, until the end time; because it is still to come at the appointed time...."

—Daniel 11

As you read these passages carefully, you will see that there is a "sanctuary fortress" (Daniel 11:31) where they evidently will be having regular sacrifices. (These sacrifices may or may not be physical sacrifices like were offered in the Old Testament times.) Once the regular sacrifice ceases, then there will be three and a half years (1,290 days with the Hebrew 360-day year) until the end.

It does not say that these sacrifices are being made in a temple, but Christ said in Matthew 24 that it was in the "holy place." Therefore, there needs to be a holy place in the nation of Israel for this to occur. Many believe, and I am one, that the Great Synagogue of Jerusalem may well be this place. It is possible that a temple will be rebuilt on the Temple Mount, but I seriously doubt it.

Let us turn our attention to the phrase "abomination of desolation." What it literally means is that there will be an abomination established that will make desolate.

The word "desolate" means "void of people" or "uninhabited." A good definition of desolate is found in Jeremiah:

> 8 "Be warned, O Jerusalem,
>   Lest I be alienated from you;
>   Lest I make you a desolation,
>   A land not inhabited."
>
> —Jeremiah 6

In the passages quoted from Daniel, we see that something is going to occur which will make Jerusalem uninhabited. Christ spells this out in a little bit different way in Luke:

> 20 "But when you see Jerusalem surrounded by armies, then recognize that her desolation is at hand.
> 21 "Then let those who are in Judea flee to the mountains, and let those who are in the midst of the city depart, and let not those who are in the country enter the city;
> 22 because these are days of vengeance, in order that all things which are written may be fulfilled.
> 23 "Woe to those who are with child and to those who nurse babes in those days; for there will be great distress upon the land, and wrath to this people,
> 24 and they will fall by the edge of the sword, and will be led captive into all the nations; and Jerusalem will be trampled under foot by the Gentiles until the times of the Gentiles be fulfilled...."
>
> —Luke 21

We see that Jerusalem is going to be surrounded by armies and, when that happens, her desolation (being void of inhabitants) will be right at hand. All the people in Jerusalem will be led away captive for three and a half years, which is the time of the Gentiles.

This has been reemphasized and the time frame is given to us one more time in Revelation 11:

> **1   And there was given me a measuring rod like a staff; and someone said, "Rise and measure the temple of God, and the altar, and those who worship in it.**
> **2   "And leave out the court which is outside the temple, and do not measure it, for it has been given to the nations; and they will tread under foot the holy city for forty-two months...."**

Forty-two months is also equal to the three and a half years, and it says that Jerusalem will be trampled underfoot for three and a half years. This is almost identical to the phraseology that Jesus used in Luke 21:24.

Thus, we see that there is a time coming when Jerusalem will be uninhabited and will be trampled underfoot for three and a half years. Those who think that the nation of Israel will remain strong through the tribulation are coming up with these false ideas because of their misconception about who Israel really is. (This subject is covered in detail in my book entitled *The Coming Climax Of History.*) Those who are so strongly "pro" the nation of Israel and Jerusalem are going to be shocked when armies surround Jerusalem and it is destroyed and becomes void of all people. However, we should not be surprised, because Christ has clearly said that this will occur. It may be different from our previous concepts, but if Christ says that it is going to occur during the time of birth pangs, then it will indeed occur just as He said. (This does not mean that I am in any way against the nation of Israel or the Hebrew people. I am simply looking at what the Bible says is coming.)

The times of the Gentiles, or the times of Jerusalem being trampled underfoot by the nations, I believe is the period of the great tribulation and I believe that the Bible says it is going to last three and a half years. It appears as though the beast (commonly called "the Antichrist," in error) will have already risen to a state of world prominence and possibly even to the state of world dictator. When the beast comes to Jerusalem and magnifies himself above God, that is when the desolation of Jerusalem will occur. This is described partially in Daniel 11:

> **31** **"And forces from him will arise, desecrate the sanctuary fortress, and do away with the regular sacrifice. And they will set up the abomination of desolation....**
>
> **36** **"Then the king will do as he pleases, and he will exalt and magnify himself above every god, and will speak monstrous things against the God of gods; and he will prosper until the indignation is finished, for that which is decreed will be done.**
>
> **37** **"And he will show no regard for the gods of his fathers or for the desire of women, nor will he show regard for any other god; for he will magnify himself above them all...."**

As you can see from the passage above, this "king," more likely a dictator, will desecrate the sanctuary fortress, he will set up the abomination of desolation, he will speak monstrous things against God, and he will magnify himself above God. From this passage, we can see that the beast will be an individual and not a system or a country. The beast will have a system behind him, but he will be a person.

The rising to power of this beast is also described in the revelation that God gave to John:

> **1** **And he stood on the sand of the seashore. And I saw a beast coming up out of the sea, having ten horns and seven heads, and on his horns were ten diadems, and on his heads were blasphemous names.**
>
> **2** **And the beast which I saw was like a leopard, and his feet were like those of a bear, and his mouth like the mouth of a lion. And the dragon gave him his power and his throne and great authority.**
>
> **3** **And I saw one of his heads as if it had been slain, and his fatal wound was healed. And the whole earth was amazed and followed after the beast;**
>
> **4** **and they worshiped the dragon, because he gave his authority to the beast; and they worshiped the beast, saying, "Who is like the beast, and who is able to wage war with him?"**

5   And there was given to him a mouth speaking arrogant words and blasphemies; and authority to act for forty-two months was given to him.

6   And he opened his mouth in blasphemies against God, to blaspheme His name and His tabernacle, that is, those who dwell in heaven.

7   And it was given to him to make war with the saints and to overcome them; and authority over every tribe and people and tongue and nation was given to him.

8   And all who dwell on the earth will worship him, everyone whose name has not been written from the foundation of the world in the book of life of the Lamb who has been slain.

—Revelation 13

In this passage we see some of the same things about the beast that we saw in Daniel. He will blaspheme God and God's tabernacle (sanctuary). He will have authority over every nation (thus, a world dictator) and he will require everyone on earth to worship him, at least those whose names are not written in the book of life.

It is when this world dictator comes to Jerusalem, exalts himself above God, and demands to be worshiped, that we will know Jerusalem is about to be uninhabited.

Did you notice that verse 5 says that he will have this status for forty-two months, which is three and a half years—the duration of the great tribulation? So we see that the beast comes to Jerusalem right at the end of the time of birth pangs and his reign will be three and a half years.

Verse 7 of Revelation 13 says that the beast will have "authority over every tribe and people and tongue and nation." Thus, we know that he will be the authority (dictator) over the entire world.

Verse 1 talks about him coming up out of the sea, or out of the waters. We know that the beast is a human—an individual—because Revelation 17 tells us what the waters are:

15   And he said to me, "The waters which you saw where the harlot sits, are peoples and multitudes and nations and tongues. . . .
—Revelation 17

Revelation 13:1 also describes the beast as having ten horns. In Revelation 17, we find out who these ten horns are:

12   "And the ten horns which you saw are ten kings, who have not yet received a kingdom, but they receive authority as kings with the beast for one hour. . . ."
—Revelation 17

This says that these ten horns are kings without a kingdom. I look at those as most likely being extremely wealthy men, who are in a kingly state, but who do not have a geographic kingdom. So it is most likely that the beast will rise to power with the ten rich men giving authority to the beast.

GET READY FOR THE BIRTH PANGS

If you believe that you are likely to see Jesus Christ return, regardless of what you believe about the timing of the rapture, then you also believe that you are going to go through the time of birth pangs. You are going to experience the coming world war, which is probably going to be nuclear. You are going to experience a famine of the magnitude that 100 percent of the average working man's salary will go to buy food. You will experience persecution, primarily from people who appear to be Christians. You will experience the spiritual war that is going to occur when Satan hits the earth with a third of the angels and vents his wrath. You will see Jerusalem uninhabited, and, hopefully, you will have a part in the gospel going to all nations.

If you will indeed be going through the time of birth pangs, my question to you is this: Are you prepared for these times? Are you prepared for a nuclear war? Are you prepared for famine? Are you prepared for persecution? As I travel all around the world and share this message with Christians on many continents, many of them say to me: "James, I'm not ready in any way. I'm not ready physically, financially, spiritually, or emotionally for those things."

The reason Jesus told you what was coming at the end of this age is because He loves you and He did not want you to be caught by surprise. But, just like Noah, I believe God wants us to be ready—in whatever way He individually tells us to be ready—for what He has warned us is coming.

I do not know what God will tell you to do to get ready for famine. I do know this: He won't tell you anything unless you ask Him, because He will not force His way into your life. God was led some people to do very little, such as to store up a few extra weeks' worth of grocery store food to get ready for famine. Others He has led to lay up a year or more supply of dehydrated food. Others he has told to create a greenhouse. Some He has told to plow up their backyard and to get rid of the grass and flowers in order to plant vegetables. Still others he has moved out to farms where they can raise their own animals and crops. But if we know that we are going to face famine, then it behooves us to fall on our faces before God and to say, "God, what do you want *me* to do to get ready for the famine?"

The same thing is true in regard to getting ready for a nuclear war, earthquakes, persecution, and so forth. The middle third of my book, *Christians Will Go Through The Tribulation—And How to Prepare For It,* deals with the area of physical preparation and delineates things that God might lead you to do to get ready for some of the things that are coming. The preparations are the same for the birth pangs as they are for the great tribulation, so the information could be very helpful.

We Christians, of all people, should be prepared. We know what is coming; Christ has told us. There is no ambiguity. There is a reason that He told us of these future events, and that is so that we could be prepared and seek God's face to find out what He would have us do to be ready. Also, one of the biggest fears is the "fear of the unknown," which applies to many situations. The fact that we know what is coming and know that God is in control of it, that alone dissipates fear. Because

He loves us, Jesus let us know what signs we can look for. So when we see these things happening, we can rejoice, for we will know that God is bringing about the close of this age, just as he said He would, and the return of Jesus is near!

SUMMARY AND CONCLUSION

As the end of this age comes, we have seen that the first major thing that will occur is what Christ called the "time of birth pangs" or the "time of sorrows." This is a period of time that precedes the great tribulation. Thus, if indeed we are living in the end times of this age, the time of birth pangs is something that Christians will go through, even if there were to be a rapture before the great tribulation.

During this time of birth pangs, we have seen that there is going to be a world war—probably nuclear—as well as famine, earthquakes, persecution of Christians, and a spiritual war with Satan and his fallen angels.

God is raising up an army to come against that satanic host—an army of overcomers. We would encourage you to be part of that army of overcomers. We will overcome Satan to the praise and glory of Jesus Christ!

The beast (world dictator) will rise to power and will begin to move toward Jerusalem. The event that will terminate the time of birth pangs and will begin the great tribulation is the abomination of desolation that will appear in Jerusalem. This will happen at a point in time when armies surround Jerusalem. Then for three and a half years Jerusalem will be uninhabited as the earth will experience the great tribulation.

The exciting thing is that Christians can be protected from much that will happen on the earth and can be absolutely protected from taking the mark of the beast. However, before we examine how we can have divine protection during the end times and real victory in Christ, we need to look at three vital subjects in the next three chapters.

3

THE NEED FOR
JESUS AND HIS POWER

We all like to hear good news rather than bad. We all like to contemplate happy and pleasant things happening in the future rather than unpleasant things. However, even above that desire, we need to be realistic.

An optimist is one who looks at things as brighter than they are. A pessimist is one who looks at things as more gloomy than they are, and a realist tries to look at things *as* they are, whether they be good or bad. For example, if someone who lived in Iran shortly before the fall of the Shah said that he believed the next years in Iran were going to be terrible ones, he would not be being a pessimist, but simply a realist.

Christians in general, and particularly Christians in America, tend to be overly optimistic. In spite of mounting evidence to the contrary, we still tend to feel there is no war that we cannot win and no problem that our technology cannot solve. Because of this same attitude, the American people in general, and the U.S. government in particular, do not really deal with problems until they become major problems. There is very little anticipation of problems and almost no long-range strategy.

Even though the previous chapter was not exactly glowing in its outline of the future, it is clearly what the Bible says is coming. You might legitimately ask how accurate these prophecies are and how much we can have confidence in them. In order to ascertain this, we need to look at the prophecies concerning the ending of the previous age.

There were 330 specific prophecies in the Bible about how the previous age would end and what the Messiah would

be like. There were actually 60 major prophecies and 270 var-
iations on those. Jesus Christ fulfilled 330 out of 330, which
is essentially an impossibility, mathematically speaking.

Let's imagine for a moment the likelihood of just five
characteristics all occurring. For example, say that someone was
going to become president of the United States, his first name
was going to be Ralph, he was going to be blonde, he would
have played football at Notre Dame and his wife's name would
be Ruth. What is the probability of all five of those things happening? Very remote, and that is with only five characteristics.

If we had 330 characteristics, the likelihood of all of them
occurring has about the same probability as if there were an
explosion in a print shop (given adequate type) and all of the
type were to fall down into the entire works of Shakespeare,
without a single error in words, capitals, or even punctuation.
The probability of Jesus fulfilling all 330 out of 330 prophecies is the same probability of such a print shop accident resulting in the works of Shakespeare.

Since the Bible was so accurate concerning how the previous age would end, we can have a high degree of confidence
in its prophecies concerning how this current age will end. We
are not talking about the end of the world, but just one age
ending and another beginning.

Just as God brought the plagues on Egypt, the Bible says
God is going to bring many plagues upon the earth as this age
is ending, *prior* to the great tribulation.

THE NEED FOR JESUS

For a person who is not a Christian (one who does not
know Jesus Christ as his personal Savior) to go through the time
of birth pangs that precedes the great tribulation without Jesus
is going to be terrible. We need to have the peace of Jesus that
will take us through any kind of trouble. Just a few days before
He was going to be tortured to death, Jesus said, "My peace
I give unto you" (John 14:27). That is the kind of peace we are
going to need during the time of birth pangs, and only Jesus
can give us that peace.

Only Jesus can give us the joy that can be with us in troubled times. After having his back laid open with many whip lashes and then being thrust into an inner prison with his feet in stocks, Paul was singing praises to God at midnight. Only Jesus can give you that kind of joy that can take you through the storms of life rejoicing and through the troubled days that lie ahead in real victory.

There are many nice, wonderful people, who attend church, live good, moral lives, and do good things for other people, yet who have never known Jesus Christ as their personal Savior. I myself was in that category. If people asked me back in those days if I were a Christian, I would always answer "yes."

When someone asked me if I had been born again, I would say, "Sure." Then some Christians asked me *when* I had received Jesus Christ as my personal Savior, and I had to answer honestly, "I don't know." Then they said, "If you don't know when it happened, how do you know that it has happened?" This was a jolt to me, but I thank the Lord, for it was the thing that began my seeking the Lord. About three months later, I received Jesus Christ as my personal Savior and was truly born again. What a difference! What I had thought was Christianity really was not Christianity at all. Being a Christian means having a personal relationship with Jesus.

If you are not *absolutely sure* that you have been born again, that you have received Jesus Christ as your personal Savior, I would encourage you to read Appendix A right now, before you proceed with this book. That appendix will help you understand exactly what it means to have Jesus as your personal Savior and to have a vibrant, exciting relationship with Him. That is the most vital question that you will ever face! If you have any doubt whatsoever, I would encourage you to stop now and read that appendix, so that you can be absolutely sure that you have Jesus Christ as your Savior.

THE NEED FOR SUPERNATURAL POWER

It is obvious that it would be far better to go through the time of birth pangs being able to utilize supernatural power than to attempt to go through it in your own strength. Supernatural power is available to all Christians, but unfortunately many of them have not come into a position wherein they can utilize it.

There is much confusion in Christian circles today about the Holy Spirit and supernatural power. If you will forgive me, I would like to start at the very beginning and examine the Holy Spirit from ground zero, just to be certain we are together. We need to look at who He is, our relationship to Him, and what He does in and through us. Let us first look at the task of the Holy Spirit.

As a teacher and speaker at conferences, it has always been very difficult for me to give a message on the Holy Spirit. The reason is that the Holy Spirit's task is to glorify Jesus Christ. It is difficult to preach about the Holy Spirit without glorifying the Holy Spirit. Yet if someone gives a message on the Holy Spirit that glorifies the Spirit, it is not *of* the Spirit; if it were, it would glorify Jesus Christ instead. This is clearly spelled out in John 16:

> **13   "But when He, the Spirit of truth, comes, He will guide you into all the truth; for He will not speak on His own initiative, but whatever He hears, He will speak; and He will disclose to you what is to come.**
>
> **14   "He shall glorify Me; for He shall take of Mine and shall disclose *it* to you...."**

I have been to charismatic meetings where the people were so concerned about the gifts of the Spirit, that the Holy Spirit was all they talked about and, I believe, the only One they glorified. The name of Jesus was rarely mentioned. I do not believe a meeting of this type is of the Spirit of God. If it were of the Spirit, Jesus would be the One being glorified.

Thus, it is my prayer and desire that this chapter, even though speaking about the Holy Spirit and His gifts, lift up our Lord and Savior, Jesus Christ.

WHO OR WHAT IS THE HOLY SPIRIT?

I hate to begin on such an elementary level, but some people think that the Holy Spirit is an "influence," a "feeling" or a "rosy glow." Not so. He is an individual—a person, just like God the Father and Jesus Christ. In fact, Jesus equated the Holy Spirit to Himself:

16 "And I will ask the Father, and He will give you another Helper, that He may abide with you forever;
17 *that is* the Spirit of truth, whom the world cannot receive, because it does not behold Him or know Him, *but* you know Him, because He abides with you, and will be in you...."

—John 14

The word used in verse 16 for "another" means "identical to" or "just like." Literally, Jesus was saying that when He went away, He would give us someone just like Himself who would be with us forever. We see later in that chapter (verse 26) that the Holy Spirit will teach us all things and bring to our remembrance the things that Jesus said. John 16:13 says that the Spirit will guide us.

According to psychologists, to be a "person" one has to have three things:

1. Knowledge
2. Will
3. Feelings

The Scriptures attribute all of these things to the Holy Spirit. Verse 11 of 1 Corinthians 12 tells us that the Holy Spirit gives gifts to Christians *as He wills.* Thus, we know that He has a will. In 1 Corinthians 2:11, we see that only the Holy Spirit knows the thoughts of God. Thus, He has knowledge. We know from Ephesians 4:30 that we can grieve the Holy Spirit and Romans 15:30 tells us that the Holy Spirit has love. It is apparent that He has feelings, as well as knowledge and a will.

So in every aspect, the Holy Spirit is a person. He is a person without a body. This is why in the earlier days He was called the "Holy Ghost." In those days, "ghost" was the term people used for a personality, or a being, without a body. Today "ghost" is reserved for haunted houses, so we use the term "spirit" for a person without a body.

Jesus said that the Holy Spirit would be our Comforter. We all need comforting at times. This has been true since we were children. If we hurt our finger or scratched our elbow, we would run to our mother for comfort. When we were dating, if we broke up with our steady, we would tend to turn to someone for comfort. Today, if a man loses his job or does not get a promotion, he will go to his wife for comfort. However, the greatest Comforter of all is the Holy Spirit, to whom we can turn and receive love and comfort, along with guidance and teaching.

The Holy Spirit is not limited to being in one place at one time, as Jesus Christ was while He was on earth. In this respect, He is like God the Father; He can be everywhere at once (omnipresent). This beautiful person, the Holy Spirit, who loves us and cares for us, yearns to teach us about Jesus and to help us become like Him!

OUR BASIC RELATIONSHIP TO THE HOLY SPIRIT

There are three relationships that we have with the Holy Spirit at the time of salvation. They simply occur, whether we want them or not. When we receive Jesus Christ as Savior and Lord, we are:

1. Born of the Spirit
2. Sealed with the Spirit
3. Indwelt by the Spirit

We know from the Gospel of John that we must be born of the Holy Spirit, or we cannot enter or even see the kingdom of God.

> **3   Jesus answered and said to him, "Truly, truly, I say to you, unless one is born again, he cannot see the kingdom of God."**

4   Nicodemus said to Him, "How can a man be born when he is old? He cannot enter a second time into his mother's womb and be born, can he?"

5   Jesus answered, "Truly, truly, I say to you, unless one is born of water and the Spirit, he cannot enter into the kingdom of God.

6   "That which is born of the flesh is flesh, and that which is born of the Spirit is spirit...."

—John 3

We see from this passage that when we ask Jesus to become our Savior and we are born again, then we are really born of the Spirit.

We are also *sealed* by the Holy Spirit. There are various types of "sealing." The one that pertains here is like placing a government seal on a document. It is a guarantee-type seal:

13   In Him, you also, after listening to the message of truth, the gospel of your salvation—have also believed, you were sealed in Him with the Holy Spirit of promise,...

—Ephesians 1

The third relationship we have with the Holy Spirit is that He comes to dwell within us. This indwelling happens at the time we receive Jesus as our personal Savior. If you do not have the Holy Spirit, you do not have a relationship with Jesus Christ, you are not "born again" and, according to the Bible, you are not a son of God.

9   However you are not in the flesh but in the Spirit, if indeed the Spirit of God dwells in you. But if anyone does not have the Spirit of Christ, he does not belong to Him.

10   And if Christ is in you, though the body is dead because of sin, yet the spirit is alive because of righteousness.

11   But if the Spirit of Him who raised Jesus from the dead dwells in you, He who raised Christ Jesus from the dead will also give life to your mortal bodies through His Spirit who indwells you.

12   So then, brethren, we are under obligation, not to the flesh, to live according to the flesh—

13   for if you are living according to the flesh, you must die; but if by the Spirit you are putting to death the deeds of the body, you will live.

14   For all who are being led by the Spirit of God, these are the sons of God.

—Romans 8

In verse 9, we see that if you do not have the Spirit of God dwelling within you, you do not belong to Jesus. Our relationship with the Holy Spirit is one that grows and progresses throughout our Christian lives. One might think that once the Holy Spirit comes to live inside of us, that is all there is. This isn't true; there is more, as we will see as we look at the first apostles.

There is some question as to when the apostles were actually born again. It certainly had to occur after Jesus' death and resurrection. After discussing this with many Christian leaders and authors, I believe that the apostles' conversion is recorded in John 20:

21   Jesus therefore said to them again, "Peace *be* with you; as the Father has sent Me, I also send you."

22   And when He had said this, He breathed on them, and said to them, "Receive the Holy Spirit.

23   "If you forgive the sins of any, *their sins* have been forgiven them; if you retain the *sins* of any, they have been retained."

At this point in time, the apostles had believed on Jesus Christ as the Son of God and had accepted His resurrection. In these verses, they received the Holy Spirit. (If Jesus commands, "Receive the Holy Spirit," believe me—you receive the Holy Spirit.) In verse 23, Jesus also gave them some measure of spiritual authority. You might think that this was all that they needed, but evidently not; there was more to come, as we will see in a moment.

Many Christians today are living in this realm. They know Jesus as their Savior and have the Holy Spirit inside of them, but they lack evidence of supernatural power.

These first three relationships with the Holy Spirit (born, sealed and indwelt) happen at the time of our salvation. However, there is a fourth relationship with the Holy Spirit that depends on us. Some Christians have this fourth relationship and some do not. However, it is this fourth relationship that is essential if we are to have the supernatural power that God wants us to have.

BEING FILLED WITH THE HOLY SPIRIT

As we have already seen, the disciples received the Holy Spirit in John 20; He came to dwell within them at that point. Yet Jesus later told these same disciples that they needed something in addition to the indwelling of the Holy Spirit:

> **4   And gathering them together, He commanded them not to leave Jerusalem, but to wait for what the Father had promised, "Which," *He said,* "you heard of from Me;**
>
> **5   for John baptized with water, but you shall be baptized with the Holy Spirit not many days from now."...**
>
> **8   but you shall receive power when the Holy Spirit has come upon you; and you shall be My witnesses both in Jerusalem, and in all Judea and Samaria, and even to the remotest part of the earth."**
>
> **—Acts 1**

In the verses above, Jesus told the apostles that they needed *power* and that they would receive this power when the Holy Spirit came upon them, when they were baptized with the Holy Spirit. The fulfillment of this is recorded in the next chapter of Acts:

> **2   And suddenly there came from heaven a noise like a violent, rushing wind, and it filled the whole house where they were sitting.**
>
> **3   And there appeared to them tongues as of fire distributing themselves, and they rested on each one of them.**

4   And they were all filled with the Holy Spirit and began to speak with other tongues, as the Spirit was giving them utterance.

—Acts 2

We see that these Christians were filled with the Holy Spirit, they received power, and they demonstrated supernatural gifts (speaking in other known but unlearned languages). As we read in Acts 1:5, Jesus told the disciples that they would soon be baptized with the Holy Spirit, and this is the fulfillment of that prophecy, when they were first filled with the Spirit. Later on in the book of Acts, many of these same disciples were "filled with the Holy Spirit" on numerous occasions. I use the term "baptized with the Spirit" to refer to the first filling of the Holy Spirit.

Some Christians are strongly against using the term "baptized in the Spirit." I prefer to use the same terms that the Bible uses and I cannot get away from the fact that this is a very biblical term. For example, it is clearly stated that Jesus would baptize us with the Holy Spirit:

11   "As for me, I baptize you with water for repentance, but he who is coming after me is mightier than I, and I am not fit to remove His sandals; He will baptize you with the Holy Spirit and fire...."

—Matthew 3

The above Scripture is what John the Baptist had to say about Jesus. As we read earlier in Acts 1:4-5, Jesus Himself told the disciples that they would be "baptized with the Holy Spirit not many days from now."

Since one of the tasks of Jesus was to baptize us with the Holy Spirit, it is all right to use that term. But, as I said, I use it to refer to the first infilling of an individual by the Holy Spirit.

I was raised as a Methodist and tended to discount (discard is probably a better word) anything concerning being baptized with the Holy Spirit. We thought that those who taught such a thing were trying to say that we needed a "second blessing" and, hence, we tended to look down our noses at them. However, now that I have grown in the Lord, I have discovered that the Bible states clearly that there is indeed something beyond salvation that God wants to give to us, and that is the baptism in the Holy Spirit. Let's read further about this:

> **14   Now when the apostles in Jerusalem heard that Samaria had received the word of God, they sent them Peter and John,**
> **15   who came down and prayed for them, that they might receive the Holy Spirit.**
> **16   For He had not yet fallen upon any of them; they had simply been baptized in the name of the Lord Jesus.**
> **17   Then they *began* laying their hands on them, and they were receiving the Holy Spirit.**
>
> **—Acts 8**

These verses tell us that people in Samaria had received Jesus Christ and had been baptized in the name of the Lord Jesus. They were born-again believers. Evidently, though, there was something they still lacked. For this reason, the disciples in Jerusalem sent Peter and John all the way up to Samaria to help them get whatever it was that they lacked, even though they had indeed believed in Christ.

From Jerusalem to Samaria is very rugged terrain. The journey by foot was long and hard, and it must have taken Peter and John at least a couple of days. Yet they were willing to walk all that distance and risk the dangers of the rugged countryside in order that the believers in Jesus in Samaria might receive the baptism of the Holy Spirit. That is how important it was to Peter and John. They should have known the importance of it, because they had walked and talked and lived with Jesus Christ.

When Peter and John got to Samaria, they prayed for the Christians there and those Christians received the baptism of the Holy Spirit. I believe it is as important for Christians today to be baptized in the Holy Spirit as it was in this incident when Peter and John went to Samaria. Unfortunately, there has been much confusion on the baptism of the Holy Spirit; perhaps I can clear up some of it, as I share with you the things that God has laid on my heart concerning it.

HOW TO BE BAPTIZED IN THE HOLY SPIRIT

The first question that arises is: "How does a Christian know whether or not he has been baptized in the Holy Spirit?" I believe that when a Christian is baptized in the Holy Spirit, something supernatural (unexplainable in human terms) happens to him or through him. The supernatural thing might be seeing a vision; it might be praying for someone and seeing that person healed; it might be prophesying, singing in the Spirit, performing a miracle, speaking in tongues or something else. I do not believe that it has to be speaking in tongues, although that is the most common manifestation of the baptism of the Holy Spirit.

The Holy Spirit will give each person whatever gift(s) He wants him to have (1 Corinthians 12:1-11), but it will be something miraculous that cannot be explained in human terms. If you have never had something supernatural happen to you or through you, there is a good chance that you have not yet been baptized in the Holy Spirit.

If you think you might have been baptized in the Holy Spirit but are unsure, I would encourage you to ask God to give you afresh a supernatural confirmation of your baptism in the Holy Spirit.

It would be hard for someone to forget being baptized in water. Being baptized in the Holy Spirit should be an even more memorable event because of supernatural manifestations. Satan is the one who tries to bring doubt and confusion about this.

If you are a Christian and you know that you have not been baptized in the Holy Spirit (you have accepted Jesus Christ as your Lord and Savior and would like the power of God's Spirit operating in your life), the logical question is, how do you receive this? There is much confusion on the subject, which there need not be.

I would like to relate something that happened to me one time when I was ministering at a church in Minnesota. Rarely do I feel impressed of the Lord, at the end of a message, to give a "come forward" invitation. Even more rarely do I ask for those who want to be baptized in the Holy Spirit to come forward. But on this one particular Sunday, I felt the Lord wanted me to do this. So I asked any of those who would like to receive the baptism of the Holy Spirit to come forward. The pastor suggested that they go into a back room, which they did. I stayed out front and counseled and prayed with a few people, and about ten minutes later I went back and joined them in this room.

What I saw there really grieved my spirit. The brother who was trying to help these people receive the baptism of the Spirit was telling them to drop their jaws, to hold up their hands, not to say anything in English, to make sounds and so forth. I thought, "Oh my! It will be very difficult to receive the baptism of the Holy Spirit this way!" So I asked the brother if I could say something. (Since I was the visiting minister, he just about had to say "yes.")

I related to these precious brothers and sisters how I had initially received the baptism of the Holy Spirit. It had occurred a number of years earlier, when I was flying from Houston to Dallas. That particular plane had a compartment up front with eight seats that was totally isolated from the rest of the cabin. I was the only one in this front compartment and I began to pray, as I frequently do on a flight. As I talked to God, I began to tell Him how wonderful, glorious, magnificent and all-powerful He was and to thank Him that He was so holy, pure and righteous. Pretty soon my human words seemed too inadequate to express what I was feeling toward God. I then began what I call "spiritual humming." (I have only heard one other Christian do this since then.) As the pitch of my hum went up, it seemed like it touched God and as the pitch of my hum came down, it was as though it touched my heart. I sat there humming from high notes to low notes, to high notes to low notes, communing with God, praising Him, worshiping Him, and adoring Him in a way that was above and beyond what I could do in English words.

After sharing this experience, I encouraged the people to get their minds off the gifts of the Spirit or speaking in tongues and just to begin to worship and praise God. I told them that when English became totally inadequate to express their adoration, God would take over beyond that.

That evening, several of these people came up to me stating that they had received the baptism of the Holy Spirit during the afternoon between the morning and the evening services. I particuarly remember one young man who came up to me with tears in his eyes. He said that for eight years he had been seeking the baptism of the Holy Spirit and that every time an invitation was given for those who wanted to receive the baptism of the Spirit, he came forward for prayer. Evidently he had been forward literally dozens of times during this eight-year period. However, he had never received the baptism of the Holy Spirit.

With tears rolling down his cheeks, he related to me how, driving home from church that morning after I had shared what God had laid on my heart, he began to praise the Lord and, as his words became inadequate, he began to fluently speak and sing in another tongue. He said that he wanted to jump and dance all over the place and had to pull his car to the side of the road and stop, because he was afraid he would have an accident. He sat there in his car for an hour singing, praising and glorifying God. He said that he was so grateful to me for helping him to get his eyes off the gifts of the Spirit and the baptism of the Holy Spirit and to focus on worshiping God and Jesus Christ and yielding completely to God.

I might relate one other incident about a friend of mine, who was a dedicated Christian but had left the church that he had been attending. His daughter started going to an Assembly of God church with a friend of hers. One Sunday morning when he picked her up after church, she had tears in her eyes and she said, "Daddy, this morning I was baptized in the Spirit and spoke in tongues." This really shook up my friend, because he did not believe that those things were for today. He went home and, after lunch, went into his bedroom alone, knelt down beside the bed and began to talk to God. He said: "God if this is of You, I want it. I want all that you have for me." As he was praying, a glorious light came upon him and he began to praise God in heavenly singing that was not in English.

In most instances in the New Testament, being filled with the Spirit is accompanied by a manifestation of supernatural power in the saints. For example, in Acts 4:31, the believers were filled with the Holy Spirit and began to speak the word of God with boldness. In Acts 7:55-60, Stephen, being full of the Spirit, saw the glory of God and Jesus standing at the right hand of God, and he was able to glorify Christ while being stoned to death. Acts 13:9-11 tells how Paul, filled with the Spirit, was able to discern a spirit of the devil and cause a man to become blind by his words.

In the Scriptures, we find that almost inevitably the filling with the Holy Spirit caused the individual Christians to exhibit some form of supernatural power (supernatural gift). This filling was also a freeing and exhilarating experience that caused them to praise and worship God in a new and higher way. Acts 2 records that the onlookers thought that the Christians there were drunk. This must have been because they were so uninhibited, free and exuberant. This analogy to being drunk is carried further in Paul's letter to the Ephesians:

> **18   And do not get drunk with wine, for that is dissipation, but be filled with the Spirit,**
> **19   speaking to one another in psalms and hymns and spiritual songs, singing and making melody with your heart to the Lord;**
> **20   always giving thanks for all things in the name of our Lord Jesus Christ to God, even the Father;**
> **21   and be subject to one another in the fear of Christ.**
>
> **—Ephesians 5**

Verse 18 is in the imperative form: "Be filled with the Spirit." This is not a suggestion, but a command. Therefore, it must be something over which we have some control. This filling is something that we can *choose* to allow to happen or not. It is up to us whether or not we yield ourselves to the Holy Spirit, that He might take charge of our minds and bodies in order to glorify Jesus in fullness.

The main point here is that supernatural power comes when we are baptized (filled the first time) with the Holy Spirit. Believe me, we are going to need supernatural power in the turbulent days ahead. We must have supernatural power to be able to heal, to cast out demons and to perform miracles like Jesus did. If you ask God for the baptism in the Holy Spirit, He will give it to you. The Bible tells us this:

> **13   "If you then, being evil, know how to give good gifts to your children, how much more shall *your* heavenly Father give the Holy Spirit to those who ask Him?"**
>
> **—Luke 11**

You can be baptized in the Holy Spirit, (filled with the Holy Spirit) right now, as you ask God to baptize you in His Spirit. This can happen wherever you are. God will not withhold His Holy Spirit from you. Ask and receive. ("You do not have because you do not ask"—James 4:2b). Then He will display whatever supernatural gifts He wants you to have and you will receive the power that Jesus promised, supernatural power.

YOU AIN'T SEEN NOTHIN' YET

In the Pentecostal and Charismatic movements, we have seen the gifts of the Holy Spirit restored. The primary gifts that have been exercised in those movements are the gift of tongues, the gift of interpretation, the gift of prophecy, the gift of healing, and, in addition, the casting out of demons. On very rare occasions, there have been instances of food multiplying. However, as the end of this age draws closer, some of the "power gifts" that were exercised by Old Testament prophets are going to be restored to the overcomers, to those who will walk holy and pure before their God.

We are familiar with Elijah calling down fire from heaven to consume the sacrifice, when he was pitted against the prophets of Baal (1 Kings 18:22-39). Also, 2 Kings 1 records how he twice called down fire from heaven to consume a captain with his fifty soldiers. This ability to call down fire from heaven falls within the category of "power gifts."

Also, we see that the prophets in the Old Testament at times exercised control over nature. For example, one prayed that it would stop raining for years and later that it would start raining again. Rivers and the Red Sea would part at their God-controlled command. Water would come out of a rock or they could call down plagues from heaven.

All of these types of power gifts are going to be restored at the end of the age. I believe the two witnesses are simply examples of what the overcomers (the bondslaves of God, the holy ones of God) will be doing and of the power they will have:

3   "And I will grant *authority* to my two witnesses, and they will prophesy for twelve hundred and sixty days, clothed in sackcloth."

4   These are the two olive trees and the two lampstands that stand before the Lord of the earth.

5   And if anyone desires to harm them, fire proceeds out of their mouth and devours their enemies; and if anyone would desire to harm them, in this manner he must be killed.

6   These have the power to shut up the sky, in order that rain may not fall during the days of their prophesying; and they have power over the waters to turn them into blood, and to smite the earth with every plague, as often as they desire.

—Revelation 11

In the preceding verses, we see that at the end of the age, these two witnesses will be able to call forth fire to devour their enemies, to shut up the sky that it might not rain, and to call down plagues upon the earth. God can only give these power gifts to those whom He can trust absolutely. If God were to give this type of power to a Christian who used it in a fleshly way for his own advantage, it would be an abomination to God.

Jesus exercised power over nature and, as we become like Him, I believe we will too (of course, under the control of the Holy Spirit):

41   And they became very much afraid and said to one another, "Who then is this, that even the wind and the sea obey Him?"

—Mark 4

The Scriptures contain many other examples of power gifts. We will give just one more here. This is the situation mentioned earlier wherein Paul dealt with a magician:

8   But Elymas the magician (for thus his name is translated) was opposing them, seeking to turn the proconsul away from the faith.

9   But Saul, who was also *known* as Paul, filled with the Holy Spirit, fixed his gaze upon him,

10   and said, "You who are full of all deceit and fraud, you son of the devil, you enemy of all righteousness, will you not cease to make crooked the straight ways of the Lord?

11   "And now, behold, the hand of the Lord is upon you, and you will be blind and not see the sun for a time." And immediately a mist and a darkness fell upon him, and he went about seeking those who would lead him by the hand.

—Acts 13

I believe that the end result of the new thing that God is going to do on the earth will include these power gifts. These power gifts will be utilized to achieve God's purposes on the earth and to bring down spiritual strongholds that are set up against God. These will be the weapons of the end-time army that God is raising up.

As the call is going out to the body of Christ to begin to walk pure and holy before God, He is wanting to give you far more supernatural power than you have experienced. But he can only give it to you when He can trust you completely— when you have yielded yourself to Him just as completely.

SUMMARY AND CONCLUSION

We have seen that we have three automatic relationships with the Holy Spirit at the point in time when we receive Jesus

Christ as our personal Savior. We are born of the Holy Spirit, we are sealed with the Holy Spirit, and we are indwelt by the Holy Spirit. Thus, every Christian has the indwelling Holy Spirit. However, that does not mean that every Christian allows the Holy Spirit to control his life or that the power of the Holy Spirit can be exercised through that individual. That depends on the fourth, optional, relationship with the Holy Spirit.

This fourth relationship, being baptized or filled with the Holy Spirit, depends on our yielding ourselves to His control. There is one baptism (the first filling), but there are many fillings. (God has much that He would like to give to His children, but some things can only be given to those who are willing to yield, to obey, and to receive.) It is when we are filled with the Holy Spirit that we receive supernatural power. This supernatural power can be exhibited in various ways, but something supernatural happens to us or through us when we are baptized in the Holy Spirit.

God wants you to have supernatural power, and you will certainly need it in the turbulent times that will occur as this age draws to a close. You will also need supernatural power if you are going to be like Jesus in healing, casting out demons and performing miracles. These are things for today and God wants to use you in powerful, supernatural ways of which you have not even dreamt.

4

IS REVELATION CHRONOLOGICAL?

As we turn from looking at the time of birth pains, which precedes the great tribulation, and the supernatural power that we can have to help us through those days, we need to look also at the rapture. The rapture is the event described in Paul's first letter to the Christians in Thessalonica:

16   For the Lord Himself will descend from heaven with a shout, with the voice of *the* archangel, and with the trumpet of God; and the dead in Christ shall rise first.
17   Then we who are alive and remain shall be caught up together with them in the clouds to meet the Lord in the air, and thus we shall always be with the Lord.

—1 Thessalonians 4

However, before we can intelligently discuss the timing of the rapture, there is a very critical question that we must address. That is, "Is the book of Revelation chronological?" If it is chronological, then we have seven seals, followed by seven trumpets, followed by seven vials (or bowls). If this is the case, the seventh trumpet (the last trumpet) would appear in the middle of the great tribulation.

If, on the other hand, the book of Revelation is *not* chronological, then it could be that the seventh trumpet is at the end of the great tribulation. Since it appears to be clear that the rapture occurs at the seventh trumpet, you can see that whether or not Revelation is chronological is an important question that we must address before proceeding.

HOW TO VIEW THE BOOK OF REVELATION

Let me use an example to help you understand how we must approach the book of Revelation. If I had a dream each night for, say, three weeks about a coming world war, and I wrote down all of these dreams, it may be that a dream one night would depict events during the middle of the war, while the dream the next night might be at the beginning. Sometimes these dreams would overlap and sometimes there would be large gaps between them. In general, they would be out of sequence. If later you were to look at my recording of these twenty-one dreams, it would be very difficult for you to develop a chronology of that world war without supernatural guidance.

I believe that that is how we must look at the book of Revelation. John had a series of visions. We do not know over how long a period of time these visions came to John. We know that the first one occurred "on the Lord's day" (Revelation 1:10), but we do not know when the others occurred.

The signal that John is starting to record a new vision is that he will usually say something like, "And then I saw," or "And I looked," or "And I heard." Frequently, he will say "After these things I looked...," which tells us that sometime after the previous vision he had another vision.

The reason that the book of Revelation has been so difficult through the centuries is that only the Holy Spirit can take those visions and rearrange them in the proper sequence. Later in this chapter we will look at possible sequences of some of the major visions, but for now I would like to share with you why I think the book of Revelation is not chronological.

THE BOOK OF REVELATION
IS NOT CHRONOLOGICAL

As I said, it is my belief, after studying this book for over forty years, that the book of Revelation is not written in chronological sequence. If it is chronological, then Babylon has to fall three times. The battle of Armageddon is described three times, and we have Christ beginning to reign upon the earth during the middle of the tribulation. I will explain each of these things from the Scriptures to help you understand why I am forced to conclude that the book of Revelation is not chronological.

A very simple place to start is in Revelation 7. This obviously describes something that happens after the great tribulation is over.

9   After these things I looked, and behold, a great multitude, which no one could count, from every nation and *all* tribes and peoples and tongues, standing before the throne and before the Lamb, clothed in white robes, and palm branches *were* in their hands; ...

13   And one of the elders answered, saying to me, "These who are clothed in the white robes, who are they, and from where have they come?"

14   And I said to him, "My lord you know." And he said to me, "These are the ones who come out of the great tribulation, and they have washed their robes and made them white in the blood of the Lamb...."

—Revelation 7

Here we see clearly that this is something that will happen *after* the great tribulation, because John was observing people who had come out of the great tribulation. In order for Revelation to be chronological, we would have to take this passage and put it after the nineteenth chapter of Revelation, because we know that the tribulation does not end until Revelation 19.

BABYLON FALLS THREE TIMES?

Babylon—a city, country or system—plays a prominent role in the very end of the great tribulation. We read about Babylon falling in Revelation 14:

8   And another angel, a second one, followed, saying, "Fallen, fallen is Babylon the great, she who has made all the nations drink of the wine of the passion of her immorality."

At this point Babylon has fallen. However, we read the following over in the sixteenth chapter during judgment of the seventh bowl:

19   And the great city was split into three parts, and the cities of the nations fell. And Babylon the great was remembered before God, to give her the cup of the wine of His fierce wrath.

—Revelation 16

Thus, in Chapter 16 we see Babylon falling again, as God pours out His wrath upon it. Either Babylon fell in Chapter 14 and was rebuilt and fell again here in Chapter 16, or both of these are descriptions of the same event. If they are describing the same event, then the book of Revelation cannot be chronological. To make matters worse, in Revelation 17 and 18 we see Babylon fall once more:

10   standing at a distance because of the fear of her torment saying, 'Woe, woe, the great city, Babylon, the strong city! For in one hour your judgment has come.'...

20   "Rejoice over her, O heaven, and you saints and apostles and prophets, because God has pronounced judgment for you against her."

21   And a strong angel took up a stone like a great millstone and threw it into the sea, saying, "Thus will Babylon, the great city, be thrown down with violence, and will not be found any longer...."

—Revelation 18

If one tried to make the book of Revelation chronological, Babylon would fall in Revelation 14, then have to be rebuilt, to be destroyed again by God in Chapter 16, and then be rebuilt, to be destroyed one more time in Chapter 18. This is not a very intelligent interpretation. What I believe we are really reading is that John saw Babylon fall in three different visions, and the content of all three visions will take place at the same time. This would be one very strong indication that the book of Revelation is not chronological.

HOW MANY BATTLES OF ARMAGEDDON?

If we try to read the book of Revelation as through it were chronological, then we have the battle of Armageddon occurring more than once. The most standard and widely accepted description of the battle of Armageddon is this:

> **17   And I saw an angel standing in the sun; and he cried out with a loud voice, saying to all the birds which fly in midheaven, "Come, assemble for the great supper of God;**
>
> **18   in order that you may eat the flesh of kings and the flesh of commanders and the flesh of mighty men and the flesh of horses and of those who sit on them and the flesh of all men, both free men and slaves, and small and great.**
>
> **19   And I saw the beast and the kings of the earth and their armies, assembled to make war against Him who sat upon the horse, and against His army.**
>
> **20   And the beast was seized, and with him the false prophet who performed the signs in his presence, by which he deceived those who had received the mark of the beast and those who worshiped his image; these two were thrown alive into the lake of fire which burns with brimstone.**
>
> **21   And the rest were killed with the sword which came from the mouth of Him who sat upon the horse, and all the birds were filled with their flesh.**
>
> **—Revelation 19**

But it is interesting that the sixth bowl also describes the battle of Armegeddon—or "Har-magedon" in Hebrew. *Har* means "mountain." "Har-Carmel" would mean Mt. Carmel. Back in Revelation 16, we have "Har-Magedon," which means "Mt. Magedon":

> **12   And the sixth *angel* poured out his bowl upon the great river, the Euphrates; and its water was dried up, that the way might be prepared for the kings from the east....**

16   And they gathered them together to the place which in Hebrew is called Har-Magedon.
                                                    —Revelation 16

If we consider the book of Revelation to be chronological, we have already had the battle of Har-Magedon (Armageddon) occur twice. Many scholars feel that the battle of Armageddon is also described in Revelation 9, because they talk about the two hundred million horsemen when referring to Har-Magedon.

13   And the sixth angel sounded, and I heard a voice from the four horns of the golden altar which is before God,
14   one saying to the sixth angel who had the trumpet, "Release the four angels who are bound at the great river Euphrates." …
16   And the number of the armies of the horsemen was two hundred million; I heard the number of them.
                                                    —Revelation 9

In addition to these passages, I believe that the battle of Armageddon is also described in Revelation 11:

18   "And the nations were enraged, and Thy wrath came, and the time *came* for the dead to be judged, and *the time* to give their reward to Thy bond-servants the prophets and to the saints and to those who fear Thy name, the small and the great, and to destroy those who destroy the earth."

When Jesus Christ destroys those who destroy the earth, I believe that is describing the battle of Armageddon.

In order to try to make the book of Revelation chronological, this major battle—which involves the Euphrates river drying up—would have to occur at least two times, and possibly as many as four times. Another possibility is that John saw the battle of Armageddon in various visions that he had, and he described it more than once. It is far easier to me to assume that the book of Revelation is *not* chronological and that John simply saw visions of the battle of Armageddon on different occasions.

In a subsequent chapter, we will see why I feel that the seventh trumpet occurs at the end of the great tribulation. At that point, we will look at it in detail, but for now, suffice it to say that the seventh trumpet contains this sequence:

> **15   And the seventh angel sounded; and there arose loud voices in heaven, saying,**
> **"The kingdom of the world has become the *kingdom* of our Lord, and of His Christ; and He will reign forever and ever."**
> **16   And the twenty-four elders, who sit on their thrones before God, fell on their faces and worshiped God,**
> **17   saying,**
> **"We give Thee thanks, O Lord God, the Almighty, who art and who wast, because Thou hast taken Thy great power and hast begun to reign.**
>
> **—Revelation 11**

In these verses we see that at the seventh trumpet the kingdoms of the world become the kingdoms of Jesus Christ. At the seventh trumpet, He begins to reign. Trying to place this in the middle of the tribulation causes incredible difficulty in reconciling that with the rest of the Bible.

SEQUENCE OF EVENTS IN REVELATION

Almost all Bible scholars who have examined the question agree that the book of Revelation is not a sequential book. We have already seen that in Revelation 7, wherein John saw the vast multitude, he was told that these were the ones who have "come out of the great tribulation." So the events of Revelation 7 record something that transpires *after* the great tribulation is already over, while subsequent chapters in Revelation discuss things that are occurring during the great tribulation.

There are three basic ways that one could view the time relationship between the seals, the trumpets, and the bowls of Revelation. The first possible view is that everything occurs in a purely sequential manner. We know that this view does not hold up very well, because Christ returns and begins to reign on the earth at trumpet 7 (Revelation 11:15-17) and the bowls of God's wrath do not occur until Revelation 16. So View 1 would be very difficult to reconcile to the Bible (see Figure 4.1 on the next page).

The second way to view these events is that there is a complete overlap, as can also be seen in Figure 4.1. In other words, seal 1, trumpet 1 and bowl 1 would all be occurring simultaneously, and so forth. The difficulty with this view is that many of the plagues happening under the seals and the trumpets are similar but much less severe than those events occurring during the bowls.

The most likely view is some form of View 3, wherein the seals (at least the first five) occur first and then the trumpets and the bowls are overlapped to some degree. We do not know if there will be a complete overlap or if the bowls might occur between trumpets 6 or 7 or if the trumpet brings a partial plague on the earth, which is followed by a bowl completing the plague around the world. If this is the case, the trumpets and bowls would alternate. We do not know exactly how these trumpets and bowls overlap, but they appear to be very similar in nature and to occur in roughly the same time frame. Since the degree of overlap of the trumpets and the bowls is certainly subject to wide speculation and interpretation, please do not take either of the possibilities shown in View 3 of Figure 4.1 as being a precise description of the overlaps, but simply an attempt to help you get a feeling of the possible time relationships between the seals, the trumpets, and the bowls.

We have already discussed the first five seals as being part of the time of birth pangs. Thus, the primary events that we will be looking at as composing the great tribulation will be the events that occur as a result of the trumpets and the bowls (or "vials," as the *King James Version* calls them).

The reason it is important to understand that the book of Revelation is not chronological is that most Bible scholars believe that the seventh trumpet depicts the rapture. If indeed Revelation is chronological and the seventh trumpet occurs in the middle of the great tribulation, we would come up with the rapture halfway through the great tribulation ("mid-

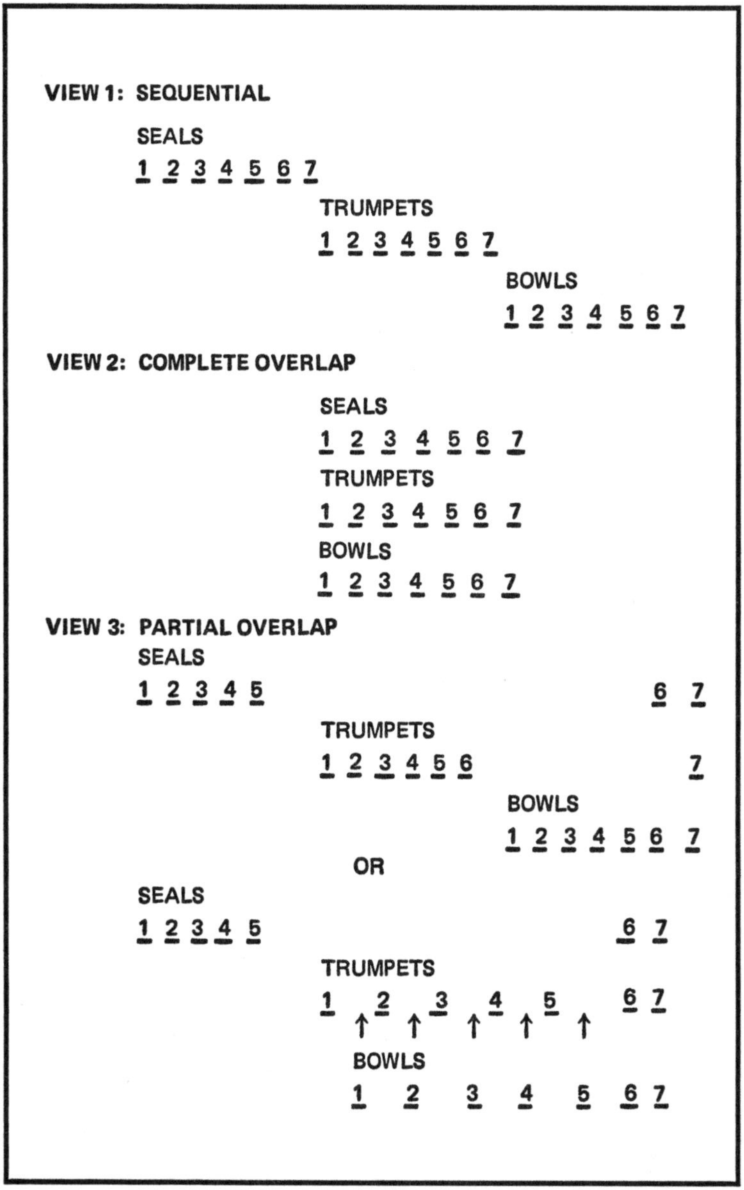

VIEW 1: SEQUENTIAL

    SEALS
    1 2 3 4 5 6 7

                TRUMPETS
                1 2 3 4 5 6 7

                                BOWLS
                                1 2 3 4 5 6 7

VIEW 2: COMPLETE OVERLAP

                SEALS
                1 2 3 4 5 6 7
                TRUMPETS
                1 2 3 4 5 6 7
                BOWLS
                1 2 3 4 5 6 7

VIEW 3: PARTIAL OVERLAP
    SEALS
    1 2 3 4 5   6 7

                TRUMPETS
                1 2 3 4 5 6   7

                        BOWLS
                        1 2 3 4 5 6 7

                OR

    SEALS
    1 2 3 4 5   6 7

                TRUMPETS
            1   2   3   4   5   6 7
              ↑   ↑   ↑   ↑   ↑
                BOWLS
            1   2   3   4   5   6 7

Figure 4.1

trib"). But if I am correct in believing that the book of Revelation is not chronological, then I would place the seventh trumpet at the very end of the great tribulation, because Christ begins to reign here on the earth at the seventh trumpet. Rather than dealing with this in general, let's now look at the details of the rapture and when it might occur.

5

WHAT ABOUT THE RAPTURE?

WHY THE RAPTURE QUESTION IS IMPORTANT

Very important questions concerning the end of this age are sometimes hotly debated in Christianity. But most frequently they are ignored. Christians like to push aside questions dealing with the end of this age in general, and the rapture in particular.

If this age is rapidly rushing to a conclusion, as the majority of Christian leaders feel it is, then it now becomes very important for each Christian to make up his own mind on these vital subjects and to try to understand more about the end of this age. Remember, we will really need God's power and victory during the turbulent days that are part of the end-times.

As we will discuss later, the reason that these questions are so vital is that the answers affect—and almost determine—so many decisions in a Christian's everyday life. For example, one's understanding on these topics can affect:

1. One's pursuit of holiness and righteousness
2. One's commitment to be a bondslave of God
3. Possibly one's occupation
4. Possibly one's living location
5. What type of church one will commit to
6. Financial decisions

As you can imagine, if one felt he were going to be raptured out before any difficult or troubled times come upon the earth, then it really does not matter where he lives or what type of work he does. It would be fine for him to go to the average church where the members are not really committed to each other or to the Lord. Likewise, he would have no concern at all about any type of preparation for troubled times.

On the other hand, if a Christian felt that he would likely go through all or part of the great tribulation—and would experience famine, war, persecution and not being able to buy or sell—his decisions in these areas might be very different.

As you can see, the subject is far too critical to ignore. I can accept it when someone says he has examined the Scriptures and feels that there is going to be a rapture at the beginning of the great tribulation (pre-trib). I can accept it when a person says he has examined the Scriptures and feels that the rapture will be in the middle or at the end of the great tribulation (mid-trib or post-trib). The Christians that I feel sorry for are those who ignore the question and say that they are "pan trib"—everything is going to "pan out all right." I believe this is a very unwise approach to the situation. Of course, God has the whole situation under control, and we are not to live in any fear whatsoever about the future. That is *not* what I am suggesting.

The Bible discusses the rapture for a reason. God wants us to examine it and understand it, not only what it is, but when it will occur. Your conclusion on this will indeed affect your life.

WHEN IS THE RAPTURE?

Let us take a fresh look at just when the rapture will occur. Many Christians, perhaps including you, have never heard an intelligent, biblically-based presentation of why the church through the centuries has believed that it would go through the tribulation. In recent history, a *new theory* emerged—the pretribulation rapture theory—which departed from the historic position of the church. This new theory began in 1830. It now appears to be waning and there is a massive swing back to the historic position of the church.

Today, there are many outstanding men and women of God who believe that Christians will go through all or part of the great tribulation. In addition to myself, among those who believe this are:

Corrie Ten Boom
Doug Clark
C.S. Lovett
Pat Robertson
Peter Marshall, Jr.
Dr. Walter Martin
Dr. Mary Relfe
Demos Shakarian
Jim Spillman

You need to know why these intelligent, truth-seeking men and women of God believe this. I would like to ask you to read this chapter with an open heart and mind, because these Christian leaders may indeed have found God's truth concerning the rapture.

If we do not have an open heart and mind, God cannot lead us into new and deeper areas of our Christian walk. As you read, ask the Lord to show you what in this chapter is truth and what is not, and then follow and believe that which the Holy Spirit shows you is truth.

Before beginning on this subject, let me say that I love and have precious fellowship with other brothers in Christ who have a different view on the rapture. Our fellowship is around Jesus, not the timing of the rapture.

Let us first define the term "rapture." This is an extra-biblical word used to describe the event wherein Christians are caught up to meet the Lord in the air, as we read at the beginning of Chapter 4. That is going to be a wonderful time and once it happens, from that time forward, we will always be with the Lord; we will never be separated from Him. Praise His holy name!

Before we discuss further *what* the rapture is and *when* it might occur, we need first to look at some commonly-held misconceptions about the rapture. The following section is excerpted from the first couple of pages of a book the Lord had me write, entitled *Christians Will Go Through The Tribulation—And How To Prepare For It.*

WHAT THE RAPTURE IS NOT

Recently I was the speaker at a typical meeting of Evangelical Christians. There were men, women, and youths who knew Jesus Christ as their personal Savior and loved Him. They knew the Scriptures fairly well. I read to these precious people the following verses from Matthew 24:

> **40   "Then there shall be two men in the field; one will be taken, and one will be left.**
> **41   "Two women *will be* grinding at the mill; one will be taken, and one will be left...."**

As you can see, these verses deal with two people doing everyday things; one of them is taken away and the other is left. I asked this group of born-again Christians to raise their hands if they thought that this Scripture was talking about the rapture, and that the people taken away were the Christians and ones left behind were the non-Christians.

How many hands do you think were raised? None, a few, many? It was 100 percent; every single hand was raised!

I might also ask you the same question. Do you think this passage is referring to the rapture of the believers and their being caught up in the air to meet the Lord? You need not raise your hand, of course. You might simply say an internal "yes" or "no."

WHERE WILL THEY BE TAKEN?

I then had this group of Bible-believing people turn to Luke, where we read the following verses:

> **34   "I tell you, on that night there will be two men in one bed; one will be taken, and the other will be left.**
> **35   "There will be two women grinding at the same place; one will be taken, and the other will be left.**

36 ("Two men will be in the field; one will be taken and the other will be left.")

37 And answering they said to Him, "Where, Lord?" And He said to them, "Where the body *is*, there also will the vultures be gathered."

—Luke 17

I also had someone in the group read verse 37 out of *The Living Bible*:

37 "Lord, where will they be taken?" the disciples asked. Jesus replied, "Where the body is, the vultures gather!"

—Luke, 17, *LB*

This is the passage that we read earlier from Matthew 24 (verses 40,41), as recorded in the Gospel of Luke. However, after stating that in each of these cases one person would be taken away and the other left, Luke records the fact that the disciples then asked Jesus *where* the people that are taken would go. Christ's reply was that they would be taken to the place where there are corpses and carcasses—where the vultures gather. (The *King James Version* and the *Revised Standard Version* incorrectly translate "vultures" as "eagles.") These people are going to be taken to the land of the dead.

The reason that all of the recent translations translate this correctly as "vultures" is because a vulture is a scavenger bird that hangs around dead bodies to eat them. On the other hand, an eagle is a bird of prey. It will not eat anything that is already dead. An eagle will only eat what it kills. The ultimate meaning of any word must come from the context. Contextually, scholars agree that the translation must be *vultures*.

This passage in Luke shows that this could not be talking about Christians being caught up in the air to meet Jesus, and yet I have heard this taught by Christian leaders, and it is believed by many Christians, to be a Scripture dealing with the rapture. What many of these Christians do not realize is that numerous leading proponents of the pre-tribulation rapture (the rapture occuring before the tribulation) do not believe that this passage deals with the rapture.

Dr. John F. Walvoord, chancellor and former president of Dallas Theological Seminary, deals with the subject in his book, *The Blessed Hope And The Tribulation:*

> An argument advanced by Alexander Reese and adopted by Gundry is that the references in Matthew 24:40, 41 should be interpreted as referring to the Rapture. These verses state, "Then shall two be in the field; the one shall be taken, and the other left. Two women shall be grinding at the mill; the one shall be taken and the other left."...
>
> Claiming that those taken in verses 40 and 42 are taken away in the Rapture, Gundry in discussing the parallel passage in Luke 17:34-37 ignores verse 37. There two are pictured in the same bed, with one taken and the other one left. Two are in the field, one is taken and the other left. Then, in verse 37, the question is asked, "Where, Lord?" The answer is very dramatic: "And He said unto them, Wherever the body is, there will the eagles be gathered together." It should be very clear that the ones taken are put to death and their bodies are consumed by the vultures. If the ones taken are killed, then verses 40, 41 of Matthew 24 speak of precisely the same kind of judgment as occurred in the flood where the ones taken were taken in judgment. Matthew 24 is just the reverse of the Rapture, not the Rapture itself.
>
> —Zondervan Publishing House
> Grand Rapids, Michigan 49506, p. 89-90

As can be seen in this quote, Dr. Walvoord—a well-known proponent of the pre-tribulation rapture theory—clearly believes that this passage in Matthew 24, which deals with some people being taken and others being left, does not refer to the rapture. These people are being taken to a place of destruction. When the Bible talks about one being taken and the other left, it is the righteous who are left and the unrighteous who are removed. For example:

36   Then He left the multitudes, and went into the house. And His disciples came to Him, saying, "Explain to us the parable of the tares of the field."

37   And He answered and said, "The one who sows the good seed is the Son of Man,

38   and the field is the world; and *as for* the good
seed, these are the sons of the kingdom; and the tares
are the sons of the evil *one*;

39   and the enemy who sowed them is the devil, and
the harvest is the end of the age; and the reapers are
angels.

40   "Therefore just as the tares are gathered up and
burned with fire, so shall it be at the end of the age.

41   "The Son of Man will send forth His angels, and
they will gather out of His kingdom all stumbling
blocks, and those who commit lawlessness,

42   and will cast them into the furnace of fire; in that
place there shall be weeping and gnashing of teeth.

43   "Then THE RIGHTEOUS WILL SHINE FORTH AS
THE SUN in the kingdom of their Father. He who has
ears; let him hear...."

—Matthew 13

As you can see in verse 41, Christ has His angels gather
"out of His kingdom" the lawless people. Jesus continues on
to be sure they get the point:

47   "Again, the kingdom of heaven is like a dragnet
cast into the sea, and gathering *fish* of every kind;

48   and when it was filled, they drew it up on the
beach; and they sat down, and gathered the good *fish*
into containers, but the bad they threw away.

49   "So it will be at the end of the age; the angels
shall come forth, and take out the wicked from among
the righteous,

50   and will cast them into the furnace of fire; there
shall be weeping and gnashing of teeth...."

—Matthew 13

You can see here that the angels are going to come and
take the wicked out from among the righteous. That is very
clear.

There are many well-meaning preachers who talk about
the two-in-the-field instance, wherein one is taken and the other
left, as being the rapture, and I have even seen a movie that
depicted this. These men do not deliberately teach error, but

unfortunately they are misleading the sheep. Clearly from the Scriptures, and even from a leading advocate of a pre-tribulation rapture, John Walvoord, we see that this is not talking about the rapture at all.

If Christians have been misled on so simple a matter as this, just think how confused they must be on more complex topics concerning the end of the age. In this book, we would like to take a fresh look at what the Scriptures have to say on some of these matters. In this chapter, the topic we will specifically try to put in a proper biblical perspective is the rapture.

WHAT IS THE RAPTURE?

As we saw at the start of Chapter 4, the basic passage of Scripture describing the rapture is found in Paul's letter to the church at Thessalonica. Let's review what he had to say to those precious Christians:

> **16   For the Lord Himself will descend from heaven with a shout, with the voice of *the* archangel, and with the trumpet of God; and the dead in Christ shall rise first.**
> **17   Then we who are alive and remain shall be caught up together with them in the clouds to meet the Lord in the air, and thus we shall always be with the Lord.**
>
> **—1 Thessalonians 4**

One of the exciting things to me is that once this event happens (the rapture), we will always be with the Lord Jesus; we will never again be separated from Him. Praise the Lord!

As we examine these two verses from 1 Thessalonians 4, we need first to realize that Jesus is not going to blow the trumpet nor do the shouting. As we will see, angels and people on earth will perform these functions. When an earthly king is coming, he does not run ahead and blow trumpets and shout; others do those things. So it will be when our King Jesus comes back.

Returning to our discussion of these two verses, we see here that five things occur at the rapture. These are as follows:

1. CHRIST APPEARS IN THE AIR.

2. THERE ARE LOUD VOICES (shout or mourn).

3. THERE IS A TRUMPET.

4. THE DEAD CHRISTIANS RISE (and get their resurrected bodies.

5. THE ALIVE CHRISTIANS ARE CAUGHT UP (with them to meet Jesus in the air, and they also are changed to have resurrected bodies).

These are the five things that occur at the rapture. However, this passage does not give us any clue as to *when* it will happen. It only tells us *what* will happen. We must then look other places in the Scriptures for the timing of this event.

As an aside, we need to realize that Old Testament saints will be resurrected at the rapture, along with New Testament believers in Jesus Christ. One of the ways we know this is that the angel said this to Daniel:

13 "But as for you, go *your way* to the end; then you will enter into rest and rise *again* for your allotted portion at the end of the age."

—Daniel 12

The Old Testament righteous saints who followed God and the New Testament Christians together compose the whole house of Israel, and it is Israel who will be resurrected at the rapture. Now, let us proceed and find out what the Scriptures have to say about the timing of the rapture.

WHEN WILL THE RAPTURE OCCUR?

Now that we have seen the five things that occur in the rapture, let's take a look at what Jesus Himself had to say concerning when this will occur:

29 "But immediately after the tribulation of those days THE SUN WILL BE DARKENED, AND THE MOON WILL NOT GIVE ITS LIGHT, AND THE STARS WILL FALL from the sky, and the powers of the heavens will be shaken,

30   and then the sign of the Son of Man will appear in the sky, and all the tribes of the earth will mourn, and they will see the SON OF MAN COMING ON THE CLOUDS OF THE SKY with power and great glory.

31   "And He will send forth His angels with A GREAT TRUMPET AND THEY WILL GATHER TOGETHER His elect from the four winds, from one end of the sky to the other...."

—Matthew 24

It is very interesting that Jesus here describes something that is going to happen "after the tribulation," and the same five things occur that we listed earlier:

1.   In verse 30, we see the Son of Man appearing in the sky.
2.   We see all the tribes of the earth mourning, which is a loud voice. (On the evening news, I'm sure that you have seen women from the Middle East screaming, as they mourned their dead.)
3.   In verse 31, we see the great trumpet.
4.   In verse 31, we see His angels gathering the elect (the Christians) from the four winds: that is, north, east, south, west. I believe these are the alive Christians.
5.   The angels also gather the Christians from one end of the sky to the other. I believe these are the dead Christians.

I believe that Christ is describing the rapture here, because the exact same five things occur, as we read about in 1 Thessalonians 4:16,17. If so, He tells us that it will happen after the great tribulation.

However, one passage in Scripture is not enough to form a basis for a belief, so let's turn to Paul's first letter to the church of Corinth.

50   Now I say this, brethren, that flesh and blood cannot inherit the kingdom of God; nor does the perishable inherit the imperishable.

51 Behold, I tell you a mystery; we shall not all sleep, but we shall all be changed,

52 in a moment, in the twinkling of an eye, at the last trumpet; for the trumpet will sound, and the dead will be raised imperishable, and we shall be changed.

53 For this perishable must put on the imperishable, and this mortal must put on immortality.

—1 Corinthians 15

Every Bible scholar that I have read says that this is talking about the rapture, since we have the dead Christians being raised and all of us putting on imperishable, resurrected bodies. However, this passage also tells us *when* this will occur. In verse 52, it says that it will occur "at the last trumpet." This is a definite timing factor for the rapture.

So let us turn and read about the last trumpet in the Bible, which is the seventh trumpet in the book of Revelation:

15 And the seventh angel sounded; and there arose loud voices in heaven, saying,

"The kingdom of the world has become *the kingdom* of our Lord, and of His Christ; and He will reign forever and ever."

16 And the twenty-four elders, who sit on their thrones before God, fell on their faces and worshiped God,

17 saying,

"We give Thee thanks, O Lord God, the Almighty, who art and who wast, because Thou hast taken Thy great power and hast begun to reign.

18 "And the nations were enraged, and Thy wrath came, and the time *came* for the dead to be judged, and *the time* to give their reward to Thy bond-servants the prophets and to the saints and to those who fear Thy name, the small and the great, and to destroy those who destroy the earth."

—Revelation 11

In verse 15 of this passage, we see the seventh angel blowing the trumpet. In that same verse, we also see the loud voices.

This shout from heaven will join the shout from earth heralding the returning King. In an earthly parallel, if a king (or general) had gone away for a conquest, when he returned, both those in his party (or army) and those welcoming him back would all be shouting. Back to this passage, we have seen the trumpet and the shout, which are two of the five things that we have learned will happen at the rapture.

Then a very interesting thing is stated: it says that Jesus Christ begins to reign on the earth as the seventh trumpet blows (verse 17), and the kingdom of the world becomes the kingdom of Christ (verse 15). If Christ is going to come down to the earth and begin to reign, He has to appear in the air. This is the third of the five things that we are looking for at the rapture.

In verse 18, we see the dead Christians being judged. They are not going to be judged while they are still in their graves, of course, so there is the resurrection of the dead Christians. We also see that the Lord is going to reward those Christians who are still alive.

Also in verse 18, we see the battle of Armageddon, wherein Jesus is going to "destroy those who destroy the earth."

If the seventh trumpet—*the last trumpet* in the Bible—had been a plague of grasshoppers or some such thing, this would all fall apart. But the Scriptures are beautifully consistent. This seventh trumpet, which occurs at the end of the great tribulation, depicts very beautifully the five things that occur at the rapture.

There are some who believe in a mid-tribulation rapture. They use the seventh trumpet as a basis for this belief, and I certainly agree that the rapture *will* occur at the seventh trumpet, whenever it is sounded. However, I do not see how the seventh trumpet could be blown in the middle of the great tribulation, because when that seventh trumpet sounds, Christ comes down to the earth and begins to reign, as we have just seen. If you conclude that Revelation is non-chronological in nature, as per our discussion in the last chapter, then this is not a problem.

So you can see from the passage in Matthew 24 discussed earlier, wherein Jesus was talking, and the description here in Revelation, which was a revelation given to John by Jesus, that Jesus clearly says that the rapture is going to be at the end of the great tribulation.

OTHER EVIDENCE ON THE TIMING

Let's look at a few other places in the Scriptures that clearly tell us *when* the rapture will occur. Revelation 20 is talking about the time immediately after the end of the great tribulation:

> **4 And I saw thrones, and they sat upon them, and judgement was given to them. And I *saw* the souls of those who had been beheaded because of the testimony of Jesus and because of the word of God, and those who had not worshiped the beast or his image, and had not received the mark upon their forehead and upon their hand; and they came to life and reigned with Christ for a thousand years.**
> **5 The rest of the dead did not come to life until the thousand years were completed. This is the first resurrection.**
> **6 Blessed and holy is the one who has a part in the first resurrection; over these the second death has no power, but they will be priests of God and of Christ and will reign with Him for a thousand years.**
> **—Revelation 20**

Here we see Christians coming to life and reigning with Christ for a thousand years (the millennium) and the rest of the dead (non-Christian dead) are not going to be resurrected until the end of the thousand years.

But the thing significant to our discussion is that this passage tells us that the resurrection of Christians here at the end of the tribulation is the *first* resurrection (verse 5). There could not have been a resurrection seven years earlier at the rapture or this would have been the second resurrection. And remember, you cannot have a rapture without a resurrection. So again, this clearly states that this first resurrection (and, therefore, the rapture) occurs at the end of the tribulation.

Moving on, when we talk about "the last days" (plural), we are talking about the time of birth pangs (which we could possibly be in now), that precedes the great tribulation, and the great tribulation itself. However, when we talk about "the *last day*" (singular), this means that the next day the millennium would begin. Effectively then that would be the last day of this age.

The next few verses that we will share may be very startling to you. I too had to read them multiple times, for I had missed their impact. Jesus Himself tells believers when they will be resurrected, if they have died before He returns:

> **40   "For this is the will of My Father, that everyone who beholds the Son and believes in Him, may have eternal life, and I Myself will raise him up on the last day."**
>
> **—John 6**

Here He clearly says that the believers in Him, who have eternal life, He is going to raise up on the very *last day* of this age (the next day the millennium will begin). Therefore, this is at the end of the tribulation. He reiterates this more than once:

> **44   "No one can come to Me, unless the Father who sent Me draws him; and I will raise him up on the last day..."**
>
> **54   "He who eats My flesh and drinks My blood has eternal life, and I will raise him up on the last day.**
>
> **—John 6**

These other two verses again tell us very specifically when he will raise the dead Christians, and that is *on the very last day of this age.*

So that you do not think this is an isolated teaching, let's look at the situation wherein Lazarus had just died and Martha was upset:

> **23   Jesus said to her, "Your brother shall rise again."**

24   Martha said to Him, "I know that he will rise again in the resurrection on the last day."
25   Jesus said to her, "I am the resurrection and the life; he who believes in Me shall live even if he dies,
26   and everyone who lives and believes in Me shall never die. Do you believe this?"

—John 11

Jesus told Martha that Lazarus was going to rise again, and she instantly responded that she knew he was going to rise on the *last day of this age.* Since she knew it so instantaneously, it must have been an ongoing teaching of Jesus. He did not correct her and tell her, "No, Martha, you are wrong; it will happen seven years before the last day of this age." Instead, He validated what she had said.

If you simply read the Scriptures and take them for what they say, they very plainly tell us that the rapture is going to occur at the end of the tribulation, on the day before the millennium begins, the last day of this age.

MORE PROOF—THE SHOUT AND THE MYSTERY

The rapture at the end of the tribulation may be such a new thought to some readers that additional evidence is desirable. One evidence is the shout (loud voices) that usually accompanies a significant trumpet blast in the Scriptures. When Jericho was conquered, we read that the seventh trumpet was accompanied by a great shout of the people:

20   So the people shouted, and *priests* blew the trumpets; and it came about, when the people heard the sound of the trumpet, that the people shouted with a great shout and the wall fell down flat, so that the people went up into the city, and every man straight ahead, and they took the city.

—Joshua 6

In 1 Thessalonians 4:16, which we quoted earlier, we see the Lord descending, at His Second Coming, with a shout and with the trumpet of God. It is exciting to discover that the seventh and last trumpet in Revelation is also accompanied by loud voices (shouts). You can reexamine this in Revelation 11:15. Revelation 14:14-20 also mentions loud voices in connection with the harvest at the end of the age.

Another factor is the "mystery," spoken of in 1 Corinthians 15:

> **51   Behold, I tell you a mystery; we shall not all sleep, but we shall all be changed,...**

The mystery that Paul refers to here is the changing that takes place at the rapture. This mystery will be finished when the rapture occurs. Right? If we are correctly interpreting the Scriptures, this should occur at the seventh trumpet. It is beautifully tied together in Revelation 10:

> **7   but in the days of the voice of the seventh angel, when he is about to sound, then the mystery of God is finished, as He preached to His servants the prophets.**

WHO DOES THE REVERSING?

In 1 Thessalonians 4:16-17, which we quoted earlier in this chapter, we saw that the Christians will "meet" the Lord in the air. The Greek word for "meet" in this passage is *"apantesis"* (which is #529 in *Strong's Concordance*). This word *"apantesis"* only occurs two other places in the New Testament. One is when Paul is going to Rome and the believers come out to meet him:

> **14   There we found *some* brethren, and were invited to stay with them for seven days; and thus we came to Rome.**
> **15   And the brethren, when they heard about us, came from there as far as the Market of Appius and Three Inns to meet us; and when Paul saw them, he thanked God and took courage.**
>
> **—Acts 28**

Here we see that the brethren came out to meet *(apantesis)* Paul. However, the principal actor in the drama, which was

Paul in this case, kept going and the people doing the meeting did the reversing of direction, as one would expect.

The only other place this word is used in the Scriptures is in the parable of the bridegroom and ten virgins. The ten virgins went out to "meet" (*apantesis*) the bridegroom. The bridegroom, who was the principal actor in this drama, kept coming, and those doing the meeting reversed course.

If this same usage holds true in 1 Thessalonians, then when we "meet" Christ in the air, He will not reverse course—we will. This is solidly consistent with the use of this word. If we reverse direction, where will we go? When we meet Him in the air, we will immediately go with Him to the Mount Zion, Jerusalem area, from which He will rule and reign for a thousand years. (As we are caught up and get our resurrected bodies, we will go with Him to Mount Zion by "TWA"; in this particular case, TWA means "Travel With Angels"!)

> **31   "But when the Son of Man comes in His glory, and all the angels with Him, then He will sit on His glorious throne.**
> **32   "And all the nations will be gathered before Him; and he will separate them from one another, as the shepherd separates the sheep from the goats;**
> **33   and He will put the sheep on His right and the goats on the left...."**
>
> **—Matthew 25**

Isn't that going to be a wonderful, glorious time, when we all are caught up in the air and get our resurrected bodies and go with Jesus and the angels to Mount Zion? When that happens, the joy we have will be with us forever and ever. We read about this in Isaiah:

> **10   And the ransomed of the Lord will return**
> **And come with joyful shouting to Zion**
> **With everlasting joy upon their heads.**
> **They will find gladness and joy**
> **And sorrow and sighing will flee away.**
>
> **—Isaiah 35**

TRIBULATION BUT NOT WRATH

Even though the Christians may experience the tribulation, they will never experience the wrath of God. All the way through the Scriptures, we are told that Christians will experience tribulation. For example, Jesus Himself had this to say to us:

> **33 "These things I have spoken to you, that in Me you may have peace. In the world you have tribulation, but take courage; I have overcome the world."**
>
> **—John 16**

Here Jesus clearly informs us that we are going to have tribulation, but He tells us to have courage; He will give us victory over the world, as He Himself overcame the world. The apostle Paul said that we would enter the kingdom of God through tribulations:

> **21 And after they had preached the gospel to that city and had made many disciples, they returned to Lystra and to Iconium and to Antioch,**
> **22 strengthening the souls of the disciples, encouraging them to continue in the faith, and *saying,* "Through many tribulations we must enter the kingdom of God."**
>
> **—Acts 14**

In his letter to the Romans, Paul amplifies on the subject of tribulation:

> **3 And not only this, but we also exult in our tribulations, knowing that tribulation brings about perseverance;**
> **4 and perseverance, proven character; and proven character, hope;**
> **5 and hope does not disappoint, because the love of God has been poured out within our hearts through the Holy Spirit who was given to us.**
>
> **—Romans 5**

Paul expands further on tribulation in a very precious way later in Romans:

35 Who shall separate us from the love of Christ? Shall tribulation, or distress, or persecution, or famine, or nakedness, or peril, or sword?
36 Just as it is written,
"FOR THY SAKE WE ARE BEING PUT TO DEATH ALL DAY LONG; WE WERE CONSIDERED AS SHEEP TO BE SLAUGHTERED."
37 But in all these things we overwhelmingly conquer through Him who loved us.
38 For I am convinced that neither death, nor life, nor angels, nor principalities, nor things present, nor things to come, nor powers,
39 nor height, nor depth, nor any other created thing, shall be able to separate us from the love of God, which is in Christ Jesus our Lord.

—Romans 8

It is wonderful that all of the terrible things that we will experience during the tribulation will not separate us from the love of Christ!

We have seen that Christians are expected to go through tribulation. However, this does not mean that we will experience the wrath of God. In fact, Paul tells us that we will not:

9 Much more then, having now been justified by His blood, we shall be saved from the wrath *of God* through Him.

—Romans 5

By negative implication, we see the same thing in John 3:

36 "He who believes in the Son has eternal life; but he who does not obey the Son shall not see life, but the wrath of God abides on him."

This verse says that those who believe in the Son have eternal life, but those who do not obey Him, not only will not have life, but the wrath of God abides on them. The implication is that those who believe in the Son will not experience the wrath of God.

The wrath of God will be poured out against the world. We can rejoice because we are not part of the world. Revelation 7:2-3 tells us that God will seal the foreheads of His bondservants to protect them from wrath (more on this exciting subject of God's supernatural protection in a later chapter). Remember, God did not remove the children of Israel from Egypt during the plagues. If they obeyed Him, He protected them from the disasters (His wrath) being poured out upon the earth. Similarly, we can go through the tribulation victoriously, by following and obeying God.

SUMMARY AND CONCLUSION

We have seen that there is a very solid biblical basis for believing that Christians will go through the tribulation or, at a very minimum, will go through half of it. However, there are sincere men and women of God who believe that Christians will be raptured out before the great tribulation begins. We need to love those brothers and sisters in Christ and to keep in mind that our fellowship is around the person of Jesus Christ, and not around any particular doctrine. I have known Hal Lindsay, for example, since before either one of us wrote a book, and I love him deeply in the Lord. I praise God for the thousands of people who have come to know Jesus Christ under his ministry. I have no lack of love for anybody who believes in a pre-tribulation rapture.

In times past, I have dealt gently with this pre-tribulation rapture theory, but now the Lord is compelling me to state plainly that it is a false doctrine. The men who teach it are not necessarily false teachers. They may be godly men, but in this area of the rapture, their teaching is false and has no biblical basis. There is not a single verse in the Bible that will support it.

A wonderful Christian pastor I know in South Africa, who had national radio and television exposure, publicly offered the equivalent of $40,000, if anyone could give him a single verse in the Bible that said that Christians were going to be raptured out before the great tribulation. Of course, he had no takers, because there isn't one.

Jim Spillman, who is a dear friend of mine and has an excellent traveling and speaking ministry, at one time believed in the pre-tribulation rapture. This was when he was pastor of a large church in Southern California. His arguments for the pre-tribulation rapture began to get weaker and weaker, so he took his Bible and some pre-tribulation books (nothing from a post-tribulation perspective) into his prayer closet and hibernated for three days. His intention was to find out from the Bible why he really believed in the pre-tribulation rapture, so that he could come out and strongly defend the pre-tribulation position. After three days alone with God and God's word, he came out believing that Christians will go through the tribulation and that the rapture will be at the end of the tribulation.

Jim told me that he could not find a single verse in the Bible that supported the pre-tribulation rapture and that he found a whole host of verses that said Christians would go through the tribulation. The next Sunday he stood up in front of his church and told them that God had shown him that what he had been teaching them about the rapture and the tribulation was not true. He then shared with them what God had revealed to him. It takes a real man of God to stand up and do something like that, and I admire him for doing so.

How I hope and pray with all of my heart that men and women of God across America and around the world will go back to the Bible itself, as Jim Spillman did, and ask God what is His truth. If we can wipe our minds clear of all of the garbage that we have been fed, I believe the Spirit of God will clearly teach us what His truth is.

Now that we see solidly from the Scriptures that the rapture will occur after the great tribulation, on the last day of this age, we can move on and look at God's pattern of protection of His people through the centuries.

6

AREN'T YOU GLAD THAT GOD DOES NOT CHANGE?

In today's world of rapid and constant change, I praise God that He is constant, that He has not, and never will, change:

8   Jesus Christ *is* the same yesterday and today, *yes* and forever.
—Hebrews 13

God's pattern through the centuries has never been to remove His people from a time of trouble and turmoil, but to divinely protect them as they went through it. Many examples from both the Old and New Testaments come to mind. We will examine just a few.

DANIEL AND THE LIONS' DEN

God could have exempted Daniel from the lions' den. Daniel was "vice-president" of Babylon and, if anyone could have gotten an exemption, certainly he could have. However, if Daniel had been spared the trial of the lions' den, God would not have gotten the glory. As it was, Daniel went through the lions' den experience, and God has been getting the glory ever since:

16   Then the king gave orders, and Daniel was brought in and cast into the lions' den. The king spoke and said to Daniel, "Your God whom you constantly serve will Himself deliver you."
17   And a stone was brought and laid over the mouth of the den; and the king sealed it with his own signet ring and with the signet rings of his nobles, so that nothing might be changed in regard to Daniel.

18   Then the king went off to his palace and spent the night fasting, and no entertainment was brought before him and his sleep fled from him.

19   Then the king arose with the dawn, at the break of day, and went in haste to the lions' den.

20   And when he had come near the den to Daniel, he cried out with a troubled voice. The king spoke and said to Daniel, "Daniel, servant of the living God, has your God whom you constantly serve, been able to deliver you from the lions?"

21   Then Daniel spoke to the king, "O king, live forever!

22   "My God sent His angel and shut the lions' mouths and they have not harmed me, inasmuch as I was found innocent before Him; and also toward you, O king, I have committed no crime."

—Daniel 6

This so impressed the king that he sent out a proclamation that glorifies God as much as any passage in the entire Old Testament:

25   Then Darius the king wrote to all the peoples, nations and *men of every* language who were living in all the land: "May your peace abound!

26   "I make a decree that in all the dominion of my kingdom men are to fear and tremble before the God of Daniel;
> For He is the Living God and enduring forever,
> And His kingdom is one which will not be destroyed,
> And His dominion *will be* forever.

27   "He delivers and rescues and performs signs and wonders
> In heaven and on earth,
> Who has *also* delivered Daniel from the power of the lions."

—Daniel 6

Isn't that wonderful? By God allowing Daniel to go through this tribulation and yet divinely protecting him, God got the glory all across the kingdom!

SHADRACH, MESHACH AND ABED-NEGO

The Scriptures also record a triumphant story in the test of the faith of three outstanding young Hebrew men, Shadrach, Meshach and Abed-nego. You may remember that Nebuchadnezzar, who was king of Babylon at the time, had a gold statue made, and everyone was required to worship it. These three young men would not do so, because that would have meant denying the true God.

Finally they were brought before the king for a trial of sorts, and here is what happened:

16   Shadrach, Meshach and Abed-nego answered and said to the king, "O Nebuchadnezzar, we do not need to give you an answer concerning this.

17   "If it be *so*, our God whom we serve is able to deliver us from the furnace of blazing fire; and He will deliver us out of your hand, O king.

18   "But *even* if *He does* not, let it be known to you, O king, that we are not going to serve your gods or worship the golden image that you have set up."

—Daniel 3

Isn't it marvelous to see the faith of these three young men—faith that God was able to deliver them from the blazing fire? Their faith in God's ability to deliver was so strong, and yet they were willing to die for the Lord, rather than worship something or someone other than Him. Of course, their faith in God made the king very angry:

19   Then Nebuchadnezzar was filled with wrath, and his facial expression was altered toward Shadrach, Meshach and Abed-nego. He answered by giving orders to heat the furnace seven times more than it was usually heated.

20   And he commanded certain valiant warriors who *were* in his army to tie up Shadrach, Meshach and Abed-nego, in order to cast *them* into the furnace of blazing fire.

21   Then these men were tied up in their trousers, their coats, their caps and their *other* clothes, and were cast into the midst of the furnace of blazing fire.

22   For this reason, because the king's command *was* urgent and the furnace had been made extremely hot, the flame of the fire slew those men who carried up Shadrach, Meshach and Abed-nego.

23   But these three men, Shadrach, Meshach and Abed-nego, fell into the midst of the furnace of blazing fire *still* tied up.

24   Then Nebuchadnezzar the king was astounded and stood up in haste; he responded and said to his high officials, "Was it not three men we cast bound into the midst of the fire?" They answered and said to the king, "Certainly, O king."

25   He answered and said, "Look! I see four men loosed *and* walking *about* in the midst of the fire without harm, and the appearance of the fourth is like a son of *the* gods!"

26   Then Nebuchadnezzar came near to the door of the furnace of blazing fire; he responded and said, "Shadrach, Meshach and Abed-nego, come out, you servants of the Most High God, and come here!" Then Shadrach, Meshach and Abed-nego came out of the midst of the fire.

27   And the satraps, the prefects, the governors and the king's high officials gathered around *and* saw in regard to these men that the fire had no effect on the bodies of these men nor was the hair of their head singed, nor were their trousers damaged, nor had the smell of fire *even* come upon them.

—Daniel 3

Again, God let these men go through this tribulation and trial, but He divinely protected them in the midst of it. In fact, they did not even smell of smoke! The only thing burned was their bonds! Hallelujah! Again, God got the glory:

28 Nebuchadnezzar responded and said, "Blessed be the God of Shadrach, Meshach and Abed-nego, who has sent His angel and delivered His servants who put their trust in Him, violating the king's command, and yielded up their bodies so as not to serve or worship any god except their own God.

29 "Therefore, I make a decree that any people, nation or tongue that speaks anything offensive against the God of Shadrach, Meshach and Abed-nego shall be torn limb from limb and their houses reduced to a rubbish heap, inasmuch as there is no other god who is able to deliver in this way."

—Daniel 3

THE CHILDREN OF ISRAEL IN EGYPT

When the children of Israel were in Egypt and the plagues came, by and large, the plagues did not touch them. God divinely protected them from the plagues. Let's just look at a couple of these instances so you can see God's protection of His people during the plagues:

20 Now the Lord said to Moses, "Rise early in the morning and present yourself before Pharaoh, as he comes out to the water, and say to him, 'Thus says the Lord, "Let My people go, that they may serve Me.

21 "For if you will not let My people go, behold, I will send swarms of insects on you and on your servants and on your people and into your houses; and the houses of the Egyptians shall be full of swarms of insects, and also the ground on which they *dwell.*

22 "But on that day I will set apart the land of Goshen, where My people are living, so that no swarms of insects will be there, in order that you may know that I, the Lord, am in the midst of the land.

23 "And I will put a division between My people and your people. Tomorrow this sign shall occur." ' "

24 Then the Lord did so. And there came great swarms of insects into the house of Pharaoh and the

**houses of his servants and the land was laid waste
because of the swarms of insects in all the land of Egypt.**
                                                    —Exodus 8

Here we see that the swarms of insects came upon Egypt,
but they did not come upon the land of Goshen where God's
people were living. You could think of it this way: Suppose
the land of Goshen were on the right side of the road, and
Egypt were on the left side. It was as though the swarms of
insects were all on the left side of the road, but none were on
the right side of the road, where God's people were dwelling.
God's protection is complete and perfect.

Let's look at another one of the plagues wherein the Lord
did a similar thing:

**1   Then the Lord said to Moses, "Go to Pharaoh and
speak to him, 'Thus says the Lord, the God of the
Hebrews, "Let My people go, that they may serve Me.**

**2   "For if you refuse to let *them* go, and continue
to hold them,**

**3   behold, the hand of the Lord will come *with* a
very severe pestilence on your livestock which are in
the field, on the horses, on the donkeys, on the camels,
on the herds, and on the flocks.**

**4   "But the Lord will make a distinction between
the livestock of Israel and the livestock of Egypt, so that
nothing will die of all that belongs to the sons of
Israel." ' "**

**5   And the Lord set a definite time, saying, "Tomor-
row the Lord will do this thing in the land."**

**6   So the Lord did this thing on the morrow, and all
the livestock of Egypt died, but of the livestock of the
sons of Israel, not one died.**

**7   And Pharaoh sent, and behold, there was not
even one of the livestock of Israel dead. But the heart
of Pharaoh was hardened, and he did not let the people go.**

                                                    —Exodus 9

Here again we see God allowing the Hebrew people to go
through some tribulation, plagues, and trials, but divinely pro-

tecting them in the midst of these things. It says that *all* of the livestock of Egypt died, but not a single one of the livestock of Israel died. God divinely protected them and He got the glory for it.

The children of Israel were divinely protected from most of the plagues simply because God, in His grace, chose to protect them. However, on the last plague—that of the death angel slaying the firstborn of each house—their protection was dependent upon their *obedience*.

PROTECTION DEPENDENT UPON OBEDIENCE

In the last plague—that of the death angel—we read in the Scriptures that if an Israelite obeyed God and sacrificed the lamb, and put the blood over the doorpost, then his family was protected from the death angel. However, if an Israelite did not obey God, then he was not protected and the plague hit him as hard as it hit anyone in Egypt.

5 'Your lamb shall be an unblemished male a year old; you may take it from the sheep or from the goats.

6 'And you shall keep it until the fourteenth day of the same month, then the whole assembly of the congregation of Israel is to kill it at twilight.

7 'Moreover, they shall take some of the blood and put it on the two doorposts and on the lintel of the houses in which they eat it....

11 'Now you shall eat it in this manner: *with* your loins girded, your sandals on your feet, and your staff in your hand; and you shall eat it in haste—it is the Lord's Passover.

12 'For I will go through the land of Egypt on that night and will strike down all the first-born in the land of Egypt, both man and beast; and against all the gods of Egypt I will execute judgments—I am the Lord.

13 'And the blood shall be a sign for you on the houses where you live; and when I see the blood I will pass over you and no plague will befall *you* to destroy you when I strike the land of Egypt....'

—Exodus 12

We all rejoice as we think of the Israelites who were protected, those who obeyed the Lord in putting the blood on the doorposts and partaking of the feast that night, as they celebrated the protection and the goodness of God. Did you ever think about the Israelites who may not have been willing to obey God? If there were those who did not obey God's instructions, I am sure they would have had rational justifications, such as, "I have just painted the front porch" or "What would the neighbors think?"

Perhaps there were some Israelites who did not obey because they were rebellious against God. Perhaps they felt God had forgotten them or was treating them badly, and they were not about to obey Him. Maybe some others were simply too busy and didn't feel it was that important. Perhaps they were going to have weekend guests or the kid's wagon had just broken; they had so many things to do that they really didn't have time to sacrifice a lamb and go through all of the Passover dinner preparation. If this were so, by this disobedience (or lack of obedience), they would have lost the life of a child who was very precious to them.

There are Christians today who would allow their rational thinking, their pride, their rebellion and their business to keep them from obeying God. We are always happiest in the end when we do obey God.

NOAH'S OBEDIENCE AND PROTECTION

Noah is another noteworthy example of the thought that sometimes God's protection is dependent upon our obedience. God wanted to protect Noah from the flood, but His protection was conditional upon Noah obeying God and building the ark. If Noah had thought, "I don't need to build the ark; God will take care of me anyhow," I am not sure that God would have had any responsibility to protect Noah. In fact, if Noah had had that attitude, you and I might not even be here! But, praise the Lord, Noah was obedient.

22   Thus Noah did; according to all that God had commanded him, so he did.

—Genesis 6

Because of his obedience, God protected Noah. There are two significant things about Noah's life:

1.   He was a righteous man (Genesis 6:8,9; 7:1) and he preached righteousness (2 Peter 2:5).

2.   He also obeyed God in the building of the ark.

It was not a matter of physical preparation *or* spiritual preparation. It was *both,* and he did both for a long period of time.

We need to obey whatever God tells us to do, no matter how ridiculous it might seem (like building a giant ark out in the backyard). If we obey God, then He can protect us in the way He chooses. Of course He can protect us anyhow, but most often:

God's protection and provision
are dependent upon our obedience

GOD'S PATTERN WILL BE REPEATED

Do you realize that God is going to repeat this pattern one more time at the end of this age? Again, He is going to protect those who are truly obedient to Him. In the next chapter, we will discuss this marvelous divine protection that will be available to you and me.

7

GOD'S BONDSLAVES
WILL BE PROTECTED

As we said at the end of the last chapter, God is going to repeat His pattern one more time, in that His people are going to go through a time of turmoil and tribulation, but they are going to be divinely protected in it:

1   After this I saw four angels standing at the four corners of the earth, holding back the four winds of the earth, so that no wind should blow on the earth or on the sea or on any tree.
2   And I saw another angel ascending from the rising of the sun, having the seal of the living God; and he cried out with a loud voice to the four angels to whom it was granted to harm the earth and the sea,
3   saying, "Do not harm the earth or the sea or the trees, until we have sealed the bond-servants of our God on their foreheads."

—Revelation 7

Since it is God's bondslaves who are going to be sealed, and thus protected from much that lies ahead, we first need to examine what a bondslave is before proceeding to look at God's divine protection during the coming turmoil and tribulation.

GOD'S BONDSLAVES

An even better title for "God's bondslaves" would probably be *"God's volunteer permanent slaves."* When we think of the word "slave," we think of people from Africa who were captured by force, taken somewhere like America and forced into slavery. We also might think of slaves in the ancient times, such as under the Roman Empire, when a country was captured and some or most of the people in that country were forced into slavery at the hands of the victors. Of course, children born to slave parents were born into slavery. Thus, our basic concept of slavery is that people are either forced into it or born into it.

It would be almost impossible for most people to conceive of a free person walking up to a slave master and volunteering to become a permanent slave. To us this would almost seem like an act of a psychotic, a masochist, or a moron. As we will see later in this chapter, that is precisely what God wants us to do. To those who don't know God and Christ in an intimate way, to do so may indeed seem like lunacy or psychotic behavior, but those who know God well realize that it is the only path to victory and an overcoming life.

THE DIFFERENCE BETWEEN
A SLAVE AND A SERVANT

Unfortunately, some of the new translations of the Bible use the words *slave* and *servant* almost interchangeably. In many instances where the word would more accurately be translated "bondslave," it is unfortunately translated "bondservant." The terms *slave* and *servant* are far from interchangeable.

A servant gets paid a wage, however small it may be. That servant then can go out and buy with that wage anything he or she wants to buy. The servant also has days off, during which he can do anything that he desires. Thus, he has control over a portion of his life. Servants may live in virtual poverty or have a low standard of living, but they are still in control of their spending and a portion of their time.

On the other hand, a slave never receives any money of his own whatsoever. Anything that he wants he must ask of his master. If he wants some new clothes, he must ask his master for them. His master may say "yes" or "no" and, if the answer is "yes," he might also specify what kind and what color. If the slave wants to take a wife, he must ask his master if he may have one. His master may answer "yes" or "no." If the answer is "yes," the master can also decide who the slave must marry. The slave has no "rights" to marry whomever he pleases. He does his master's bidding. If the slave wants to live in a different house, have a piece of furniture or anything else, he cannot make the decision himself for he has no money to purchase these items; he must go to the master and ask him, and then do whatever the master says or receive whatever the master gives.

Similarly, there is never any time at all when the slave is not a slave. He doesn't have any "days off." His time is 100 percent under the control of his master. He may be dead tired and need a vacation, but if his master says, "Work," he works. He may be sick, but if his master tells him to do something, the slave must do it, in spite of his sickness. *His time is not his own.*

In the time of the feudal lords where there were feudal slaves, the slaves were used as part of the army of the feudal lord in the event of any attack. Thus, if a master told a slave to go out into battle and charge up a particular hill, the slave had to do it, even if it meant his death. For a person to voluntarily become a slave, he was voluntarily making a commitment to die for his master, if his master wanted him to die.

From that time on, he would have no possessions, except what the master gave him, no discretionary spending money of his own, no time of his own and no rights at all. As you can see, being a slave is far, far different from being a servant. If one is a servant, one can quit whenever one wants to. If one is a slave, one can never quit.

Now let's take a look at bondslaves in the Old Testament, then bondslaves in the New Testament, and after that we will examine what implications being a bondslave has for you and me.

A BONDSLAVE IN THE OLD TESTAMENT

The concept of a bondslave (a voluntary permanent slave) in the Old Testament is found in numerous places. One of the best descriptions of it is in Deuteronomy:

> **12** **"If your kinsman, a Hebrew man or woman, is sold to you, then he shall serve you six years, but in the seventh year you shall set him free.**
>
> **13** **"And when you set him free, you shall not send him away empty-handed.**
>
> **14** **"You shall furnish him liberally from your flock and from your threshing floor and from your wine vat; you shall give to him as the LORD your God has blessed you.**
>
> **15** **"And you shall remember that you were a slave in the land of Egypt, and the LORD your God redeemed you; therefore I command you this today.**
>
> **16** **"And it shall come about if he says to you, 'I will not go out from you,' because he loves you and your household, since he fares well with you;**
>
> **17** **then you shall take an awl and pierce it through his ear into the door, and he shall be your servant forever. And also you shall do likewise to your maidservant.**
>
> **18** **"It shall not seem hard to you when you set him free, for he has given you six years *with* double the service of a hired man; so the LORD your God will bless you in whatever you do...."**
>
> **—Deuteronomy 15**

As you can see in this passage, if a person came to be your temporary slave, for whatever reason—whether because he owed you money or because he sold himself to you to raise money—on the seventh year, you were to set him free. When you set him free, you were to give him some of your material possessions so that he did not go away empty-handed.

On the other hand, he could say to you that he did not want to go away and be free again, but instead he wanted to voluntarily become your permanent slave (bondslave). If he told you that, you would stand him against the doorpost and pierce his ear with an awl, a large nail or something of that nature. The pierced ear was the mark of a permanent slave. Since he was not born into slavery, but he voluntarily became a permanent slave, he was called a bondslave.

I used to think of this passage only from the master's viewpoint. He had gotten a slave for life who would have to do his bidding, work for him, fight for him and even die for him. But as the Lord showed it to me from the slave's side, I realized that the master was also taking on the obligation and responsibility to care for that slave for the rest of his life, to protect him and to provide for him. It requires a two-sided commitment, the master and the slave each committing themselves to the other and each assuming a certain responsibility.

What would cause an individual to voluntarily become a permanent slave? One certainly would not want to do so if the master were cruel, harsh or unjust. However, if the master were loving, kind, considerate and just, and if serving him were a joy, one might well consider being a voluntary permanent slave. Even though a slave might live in material luxury, he still had no freedoms of his own.

This concept of voluntarily becoming a permanent slave, because of love for the master, is also recorded in Exodus:

1   "Now these are the ordinances which you are to set before them.

2   "If you buy a Hebrew slave, he shall serve for six years; but on the seventh he shall go out as a free man without payment.

3   "If he comes alone, he shall go out alone; if he is the husband of a wife, then his wife shall go out with him.

4   "If his master gives him a wife, and she bears him sons or daughters, the wife and her children shall belong to her master, and he shall go out alone.

5   "But if the slave plainly says, 'I love my master, my wife and my children; I will not go out as a free man.'

6   then his master shall bring him to God, then he shall bring him to the door or the doorpost. And his

master shall pierce his ear with an awl; and he shall serve him permanently...."

—Exodus 21

I think this is a very beautiful passage, because the temporary slave plainly says that he is staying because he loves his master. As we consider making God our Master, He is so loving and kind that it is easy to love Him. A better Master cannot be found!

This passage also clearly affirms that even a temporary slave had no rights at all. If the master had given the slave a wife and they had children, the wife and children still belonged to the master. If the slave decided to leave, he had to leave his wife and children with the master. As you can see, when one is a slave, everything that person has, including his wife (or her husband) and children, belong to the master and not to the slave. Yet that is a termporary condition of one who is a temporary slave, but if one volunteers to become a permanent slave, that becomes a permanent condition.

SLAVES VERSUS SERVANTS

If you are interested in studying the difference between *servant* and *slave* in the original languages, this section is for you. In the Hebrew of the Old Testament, there are two distinct words for servant and slave, a servant being one who is hired and a slave being one who does not receive wages, and who is more of a possession of his master.

The Hebrew word for "servant" is *"sakiyr."* James Strong gives the definition of this word as:

> **"sakiyr,** a man *at wages* by the day or year:—hired (man, servant), hireling."

—Strong's Exhaustive Concordance, 7916
Word Books, Waco, Texas

This Hebrew word *sakiyr* is found in such places as Leviticus 22. In the *New American Standard Bible*, it has been translated as "hired man" in this instance:

10   No layman, however, is to eat the holy *gift*; a sojourner with the priest or a hired man shall not eat of the holy *gift*.

—Leviticus 22

On the other hand, the Hebrew word for "slave" or a "person in bondage" (which implies slavery) is "*'ebed*" (5650 in *Strong's Exhaustive Concordance*). *Strong's* gives the definition of *'ebed* as:

> "**'ebed,** a *servant:* x bondage, bondman, [bond-] servant, (man-) servant."

Whenever the Old Testament talks about being a "bond-servant," the Hebrew word *'ebed* is used. This really means a servant who is not hired, but one who is indeed a slave, in permanent or semi-permanent bondage to his master.

Turning to the New Testament, again we find that there are distinct words for slave and for servant. The word for a slave or bondslave is "*doulos*" and the two Greek words for servant are "*oiketes*," and "*therapon*." Both of these latter words have the concept of a hired servant. *Oiketes* is defined as:

> "**oiketes**; a fellow *resident*, i.e, menial *domestic*:— (household) servant."

> **—*Strong's*, 3610**

In the original language, this word is used in passages such as the following. Here it has been translated "servant":

4   Who are you to judge the servant of another? To his own master he stands or falls; and he will, for the Lord is able to make him stand.

—Romans 14

13   "No servant can serve two masters; for either he will hate the one, and love the other, or else he will hold to one, and despise the other. You cannot serve God and mammon."

—Luke 16

The other word for a hired servant in New Testament Greek, *therapon*, is defined as:

"**therapon**; a menial attendant (as if cherishing):— servant."

—*Strong's*, 2324

This is used rarely in the New Testament, as in Hebrews 3:

5   Now Moses was faithful in all His house as a servant, for a testimony of those things which were to be spoken later;...

However, the Greek word for slave or bondslave, *doulos*, is defined as:

"**doulos**; a *slave* (lit. or fig., invol. or vol.; frequently therefore in a qualified sense of *subjection* or *subserviency*):—bond (-man), servant."

—*Strong's*, 1401

This is the word used whenever the New Testament talks of Paul being a bondslave of Christ or any other time slavery is mentioned. Now let's look in detail at some of the instances in the New Testament where someone was a "doulos of God" or a slave of God or of Christ.

BONDSLAVES IN THE NEW TESTAMENT

We find many examples of people who were called bondslaves of God in the New Testament. One of the first and most beautiful is found in Luke:

25   And behold, there was a man in Jerusalem whose name was Simeon; and this man was righteous and devout, looking for the consolation of Israel; and the Holy Spirit was upon him.

26   And it had been revealed to him by the Holy Spirit that he would not see death before he had seen the Lord's Christ.

27   And he came in the Spirit into the temple; and when the parents brought in the child Jesus, to carry out for Him the custom of the Law,

28   then he took Him into his arms, and blessed God, and said,

29 "Now Lord, Thou dost let Thy bond-
         servant depart
         In peace, according to Thy word;
30 For my eyes have seen Thy salvation,
31 Which Thou has prepared in the presence
         of all peoples,
32 A LIGHT OF REVELATION TO THE
         GENTILES
         And the glory of Thy people Israel."

33 And His father and mother were amazed at the
things which were being said about Him.

34 And Simeon blessed them, and said to Mary His
mother, "Behold, this *Child* is appointed for the fall and
rise of many in Israel, and for a sign to be opposed—

35 and a sword will pierce even your own soul—to
the end that thoughts from many hearts may be revealed."

—Luke 2

Where Simeon refers to himself as a "bond-servant" in this
translation (verse 29), it really should be translated "bondslave,"
as discussed earlier. What are some of the things that we can
discern about being a bondslave by looking at Simeon's life?

1. He was righteous.
2. He was devout.
3. The Holy Spirit was upon him.
4. The Holy Spirit revealed things to him.
5. He could give blessings in the name of God.
6. He could prophesy in the name of God.

Here is a picture of a pure, holy, righteous, devoted man
of God, who had the gifts of the Spirit functioning through
him.

PAUL, A BONDSLAVE OF CHRIST

Another New Testament example, in this case said to be
a bondslave of Christ rather than a bondslave of God, is the

apostle Paul. We find this mentioned several places in the New Testament:

> **1   Paul, a bond-servant of Christ Jesus, called *as* an apostle, set apart for the gospel of God,...**
>
> —**Romans 1**

> **10   For am I now seeking the favor of men, or of God? Or am I striving to please men? If I were still trying to please men, I would not be a bond-servant of Christ.**
>
> —**Galatians 1**

> **1   Paul and Timothy, bond-servants of Christ Jesus, to all the saints in Christ Jesus who are in Philippi, including the overseers and deacons:...**
>
> —**Philippians 1**

These verses shed some additional light on what a bondslave of Christ is. In Romans 1:1 we see that a bondslave of Christ is set apart for the gospel of God—or we could say "sanctified" for the gospel of God.

In Galatians 1:10, we learn that a bondslave of Christ strives only to please Christ and not to please men. His aim is to do that which will glorify Christ, even if it makes him unpopular with men.

ONLY THE BONDSLAVES ARE SEALED

As we discussed in the last chapter, God's pattern through the ages has not been to take His people out of a time of turmoil, but to protect them as they went through it. We made mention of Daniel in the lions' den, Shadrach, Meshach and Abed-nego in the fiery furnace, and the children of Israel during the plagues in Egypt. In addition to the instances we noted, there are many other people whom God allowed to go through a time of turbulence or persecution, but whom He protected in it.

The Bible says that this pattern of God's protection is going to repeat itself once again.

1   After this I saw four angels standing at the four corners of the earth, holding back the four winds of the earth, so that no wind should blow on the earth or on the sea or on any tree.

2   And I saw another angel ascending from the rising of the sun, having the seal of the living God; and he cried out with a loud voice to the four angels to whom it was granted to harm the earth and the sea,

3   saying, "Do not harm the earth or the sea or the trees, until we have sealed the bond-servants of our God on their foreheads."

—Revelation 7

Here we see that God stops the things occurring on the earth and seals His bondslaves on their foreheads. It does not say that He seals all Christians on their foreheads, only the bondslaves—those obedient ones.

We might ask what the purpose of this seal is. We find the answer to this in Revelation 9:

2   And he opened the bottomless pit; and smoke went up out of the pit, like the smoke of a great furnace; and the sun and the air were darkened by the smoke of the pit.

3   And out of the smoke came forth locusts upon the earth; and power was given them, as the scorpions of the earth have power.

4   And they were told that they should not hurt the grass of the earth, nor any green thing, nor any tree, but only the men who do not have the seal of God on their foreheads.

We see that the purpose of the seal of God is for protection. The locusts, with a sting like scorpions, can hurt all the men on earth except those who have the seal of God on their foreheads.

I covered this concept in detail in my book, *Revelation For Laymen*. I have also pointed out that Christians really do not need to worry about taking on the mark of the beast. What we should be concerned about is being a bondslave and getting sealed on our foreheads. Once God seals us on our foreheads, neither Satan, the antichrist nor anyone else can remove God's seal and replace it with the mark of the beast (the mark of the beast comes later in the book of Revelation, in Chapter 13). "Greater is He who is in you than he who is in the world" (1 John 4:4b). So our main concern should be to be a bondslave. As a result, we can be sure that we will be sealed and protected from much that is going to happen on the earth during the end times of this age.

JESUS CHRIST WAS A BONDSLAVE OF GOD

If you stop to think about it, you realize that Christ was indeed a bondslave of God. He came to do the Father's will and not His own, and His basic desire in life was to please the Father. The extent to which He was a bondslave is beautifully pointed out in this passage:

5   Have this attitude in yourselves which was also in Christ Jesus,

6   who, although He existed in the form of God, did not regard equality with God a thing to be grasped,

7   but emptied Himself, taking the form of a bondservant, *and* being made in the likeness of men.

8   And being found in appearance as a man, he humbled Himself by becoming obedient to the point of death, even death on a cross.

—Philippians 2

We see that Christ was equal with God and in the form of God, but He did not selfishly cling to that. Verse 7 of Philippians 2 tells us that He was willing to empty Himself of all of His divine privileges, to be made a man and to voluntarily become a bondslave of God. Then verse 8 says that as a bondslave of God He humbled Himself and was obedient (characteristics of a bondslave). His obedience was to the extent that He was willing to die for His Master (God) and even endure the horrible death by torture on a cross. What an incredible sacrifice He made to come from being in heaven with God, with all the power of God, to being a bondslave of God, obedient even to the point of being willing to be tortured to death! He did all of this because He loves you and me and He knew that there was no way we could spend eternity with God other than through His precious death. If Jesus Christ was a bond-slave of God, and if we truly want to become like Jesus, then we too will gladly make a bondslave commitment to God. 1 John 2:6 tells us that we ought to "walk in the same manner as He walked."

SUMMARY AND CONCLUSION

Up to this point in the book, we have seen that all Christians are going to go through the time of birth pangs. This is true, regardless of when the rapture may occur. We also looked at the fact that, when viewed objectively without any preconceived notions, the Scriptures really teach that Christians will go through the entire tribulation.

But the good news is that if we are bondslaves of God, we will be divinely protected through much of the troubled times that are coming upon the earth, just as Daniel was protected in the lions' den; Shadrach, Meshach and Abed-nego were protected in the fiery furnace; and the children of Isreal were protected from the plagues in Egypt. As with Noah and Jonah, this time our protection is going to be dependent upon our obedience to God. In reality, perfect obedience to Him is becoming His bondslave.

If God is speaking to your heart that you should be His bondslave, you may wish to use the "Bondslave Commitment" on the next to last page of this book to seal that decision right now. This is such an important step that I would encourage you to take it now while the Holy Spirit is speaking to you.

Every interpretation of prophecy has some problems. If any one interpretation had no problems, then everyone would believe it. However, if one interpretation (such as the pre-tribulation rapture theory) has a vast number of problems and another interpretation (the post-tribulation view) only has two or three problems, I would tend to go with the interpretation that has only a few problems. We want to be realistic and open before the Lord, so in the next chapter, we will look at the three problems that some Christians would attribute to the post-tribulation view of the rapture.

8

POINTS FOR THE PRE-TRIBULATION RAPTURE THEORY

The pre-tribulation rapture theory is not without any basis; otherwise, intelligent men of God would not have subscribed to it. There are three passages of Scripture that might tend to lead one to conclude that the rapture will occur at the beginning of the tribulation. These are:

2 Thessalonians 2:1-10
Revelation 3:10
Matthew 24:42-44

Even though these are the most difficult passages to reconcile to a post-tribulation rapture, I believe that the Holy Spirit has given me some insights that might be helpful. I should also add that to build a belief that one will escape the tribulation on these three passages alone, none of which are direct and explicit, I believe is building on shaky or sandy ground. Without further ado, let's look at each of these passages.

2 THESSALONIANS 2:1-10—
THE RESTRAINER REMOVED

Those who hold to the pre-tribulation rapture theory believe that this passage implies that the Holy Spirit will be removed from the earth before the antichrist appears. They reason that if the Holy Spirit is removed, the Christians must also be removed. As you read this passage, you will notice that the Holy Spirit is not mentioned directly. Before commenting further, let's read these verses:

1   Now we request you, brethren, with regard to the coming of our Lord Jesus Christ, and our gathering together to Him,

2   that you may not be quickly shaken from your composure or be disturbed either by a spirit or a message or a letter as if from us, to the effect that the day of the Lord has come.

3   Let no one in any way deceive you for *it will not come* unless the apostasy comes first, and the man of lawlessness is revealed, the son of destruction,

4   who opposes and exalts himself above every so-called god or object of worship, so that he takes his seat in the temple of God, displaying himself as being God.

5   Do you not remember that while I was still with you, I was telling you these things?

6   And you know what restrains him now, so that in his time he may be revealed.

7   For the mystery of lawlessness is already at work; only he who now restrains *will do so* until he is taken out of the way.

8   And then that lawless one will be revealed whom the Lord will slay with the breath of His mouth and bring to an end by the appearance of His coming;

9   *that is*, the one whose coming is in accord with the activity of Satan, with all power and signs and false wonders,

10   and with all the deception of wickedness for those who perish, because they did not receive the love of the truth so as to be saved.

—2 Thessalonians 2

To begin with, the Coming of our Lord mentioned in verse 1 here is the same Second Coming of Christ referred to in 2 Thessalonians 1:6-10. If you read Chapters 1 and 2 of 2 Thessalonians in sequence, as you would read a letter, you will see that Paul is talking about one event, the return of Christ in power and glory at the end of the age. The passage in Chapter 1 clearly says that when Jesus Christ returns from heaven, it will be in flaming fire, dealing out retribution to those who do not know God and obey the gospel of Jesus. Thus, we are talking about His return at the end of the tribulation. Verse 3 of 2 Thessalonians 2 says that this will not occur before two things happen:

1. Apostasy comes
2. The man of lawlessness is revealed

Verse 7 is the key. It says that the "mystery of lawlessness is already at work; only he who now restrains will do so until he is taken out of the way." I do not believe that the restrainer is the Holy Spirit nor that He will be taken during the tribulation. One reason for this is that there will be people who become Christians during the tribulation. The Bible says that no one can come to Christ unless the Spirit draws him. We also see the Holy Spirit empowering the two witnesses during the tribulation (Revelation 11:3-12). Since the Scriptures clearly teach that there will be Christians here on the earth during the tribulation, it is unthinkable, at least to me, that God would remove the Holy Spirit from them or leave Christians without the Holy Comforter. Thus, we must conclude that the Holy Spirit is alive and well here on planet earth during that time.

In his book, *The Church and The Tribulation* (published by Zondervan Publishing House), Robert H. Gundry devotes an entire chapter (8) to this passage in 2 Thessalonians 2. He points out that various writers have felt the restrainer was God, the antichrist or Satan. Some believe that what is now restrained is the appearance of the antichrist or the mystery of lawlessness. What Gundry is pointing out is that God's power is today restraining the antichrist or possibly Satan is doing the restraining. In Revelation 7:2-3 (quoted at the beginning of Chapter 7), we see God acting as a restrainer, when He commands a restraint from further destruction on the earth until the bond-slaves have been sealed. Someday the restraint will be lifted and lawlessness and the lawless one will come forth in full force upon the earth.

There is little reason to think that the restrainer is the Holy Spirit. I certainly could not subscribe to a theological system that "guesses" that the restrainer is the Holy Spirit and that someday He will be removed from the earth.

REVELATION 3:10—
KEPT FROM THE HOUR OF TRIAL

Revelation 3:10 is part of Christ's letter to the church of Philadelphia. Much of this letter was written specifically to the Christians at Philadelphia and may or may not be applicable to all Christians of all time. Christ says this in verse 10:

> **10   'Because you have kept the word of My persever-ance, I also will keep you from the hour of testing, that *hour* which is about to come upon the whole world, to test those who dwell upon the earth....'**
>
> **—Revelation 3**

The problem here is that it says that He will keep us from the "hour" of testing (or temptation). In his book, *The Blessed Hope*, George Ladd comments so beautifully on these verses that I would like to present his thoughts:

> The language of this verse, taken by itself, could be inter-preted to teach complete escape from the coming hour of tribu-lation. The language is, "I will keep thee *out* of the hour of trial" (*tereso ek*).
>
> This language, however, neither asserts nor demands the idea of bodily removal from the midst of the coming trial. This is proven by the fact that precisely the same words are used by our Lord in His prayer that God would keep His disciples "out of the evil" (*tereses ek tou ponerou*, Jn. 17:15). In our Lord's prayer, there is no idea of bodily removal of the disciples from the evil world but of preservation from the power of evil even when they are in its very presence. A similar thought occurs in Galatians 1:4, where we read that Christ gave Himself for our sins to deliver us from (literally, "out of," *ek*) this present evil age. This does not refer to a physical removal from the age but to deliverance from its power and control. "This age" will not pass away until the return of Christ.
>
> In the same way, the promise of Revelation 3:10 of being kept *ek* the hour of trial need not be a promise of a removal from the very physical presence of tribulation. It is a promise of preservation and deliverance in and through it. This verse nei-ther asserts that the Rapture is to occur before the tribulation,

nor does its interpretation require us to think that such a removal is intended.

—Wm. B. Eerdmans Publishing Company,
255 Jefferson Ave. S.E.
Grand Rapids, MI 49502, pp. 85-86

One could legitimately conclude that Revelation 3:10 applied just to the church at Philadelphia, and not to us. Or, as Ladd points out, one could conclude that it does not imply our removal from the scene.

MATTHEW 24:42-44—
THE LORD'S COMING WILL BE A SURPRISE

The suddenness of the return of Jesus Christ, or its surprise aspect, is mentioned several places in the Scriptures. I have simply chosen the one in Matthew as an example of this:

42 **"Therefore be on the alert, for you do not know which day our Lord is coming.**
43 **"But be sure of this, that if the head of the house had known at what time of the night the thief was coming, he would have been on the alert and would not have allowed his house to be broken into.**
44 **"For this reason you be ready too; for the Son of Man is coming at an hour when you do not think *He will.*..."**

—Matthew 24

The thrust of this admonition in Matthew 24 is that we should always be on the alert, watchful and ready for the return of Jesus Christ. I believe that this applies more to us today than to any Christians who have ever lived, since we probably are living in the end times of this age.

However, the problem people raise in reconciling this to a post-tribulation rapture is that we would know that Christ was coming back seven (or three and a half) years after the tribulation began, and therefore it would not be sudden or take us by surprise. This could possibly be true if we were to know exactly when the tribulation started and if we knew for sure that it was going to be exactly seven years in length. However, I do not think that we will know exactly when the tribulation begins, nor is it clearly stated that it will be seven years in length. There is considerable scriptural support for believing that it will be three and a half years in duration.

Christians should be able to discern the times and seasons and possibly get a rough idea as to when Christ might return. Remember, Noah wasn't surprised by the flood and Lot wasn't surprised by the destruction of Sodom, although they did not know exactly when these things were coming. However, to the vast masses of people on the earth, Christ's return at the end of the tribulation will be like a "bolt out of the blue."

1   Now as to the times and the epochs, brethren, you have no need of anything to be written to you.

2   For you yourselves know full well that the day of the Lord will come just like a thief in the night.

3   While they are saying, "Peace and safety!" then destruction will come upon them suddenly like birth pangs upon a woman with child; and they shall not escape.

4   But you, brethren, are not in darkness, that the day should overtake you like a thief;

5   for you are all sons of light and sons of day. We are not of night nor of darkness;

6   so then let us not sleep as others do, but let us be alert and sober.

—1 Thessalonians 5

This passage directly follows 1 Thessalonians 4:15-18, which describes the return of Christ to the earth. Paul makes a distinction between the "brethren," or "sons of light," and those who are "of darkness." He tells us that the day of Christ's return should not overtake us (Christians) as a thief in the night (verse 4), the way it will all those who do not believe and heed the Scriptures.

We Christians will be like the virgins with oil in their lamps waiting for the bridegroom (Matthew 25:1-13). They did not know exactly the hour when he was coming. They did know the season and they had to be ready continuously. I believe that this is a beautiful example of what we should be like as we await Christ's return.

THE ELECT ARE HERE
DURING THE TRIBULATION

It is obvious from the teachings of Jesus Christ Himself that His "elect" will be here during the great tribulation:

21   for then there will be a great tribulation, such as has not occurred since the beginning of the world until now, nor ever shall.

22   "And unless those days had been cut short, no life would have been saved; but for the sake of the elect those days shall be cut short.

23   "Then if anyone says to you, 'Behold, here is the Christ,' or 'There *He is,*' do not believe *him*.

24   "For false Christs and false prophets will arise and will show great signs and wonders, so as to mislead, if possible, even the elect...."

—Matthew 24

Here we see, in both verses 22 and 24, that Christ's "elect" will be here during the tribulation. Jesus says that for the sake of the elect, the days of the great tribulation will be cut short. We have no idea by how much time. This is another reason why we will not know exactly when Christ will return, but we will know the general season.

There are some who would claim that the "elect" are not Christians. However, the primary use of the word "elect" in the New Testament is to depict Christians. Jesus Himself used "elect" to mean believers in Him in His teaching about prayer:

3   "And there was a widow in that city, and she kept coming to him, saying, 'Give me legal protection from my opponent.'

4   "And for a while he was unwilling; but afterward he said to himself, 'Even though I do not fear God nor respect man,

5   yet because this widow bothers me, I will give her legal protection, lest by continually coming she wear me out."

> 6   And the Lord said, "Hear what the unrighteous judge said;
>
> 7   now shall not God bring about justice for His elect, who cry to Him day and night, and will He delay long over them?
>
> 8   "I tell you that He will bring about justice for them speedily. However, when the Son of Man comes, will He find faith on the earth?"
>
> —Luke 18

In this passage from Luke, we see that the "elect" are the ones who cry to God, those whom Jesus will find having faith, when He returns.

We see that Paul used the term "elect" to mean Christians:

> 12   Put on therefore, as the elect of God, holy and beloved, bowels of mercies, kindness, humbleness of mind, meekness, longsuffering;...
>
> —Colossians 3, *KJV*

> 1   Paul, a servant of God, and an apostle of Jesus Christ, according to the faith of God's elect, and the acknowledging of the truth which is after godliness;...
>
> —Titus 1, *KJV*

In the two verses above, we see that Paul used that term to refer to other Christians and even to himself. In writing to the Romans, he clearly used God's "elect" to mean Christians:

> 31   What then shall we say to these things? If God is for us, who is against us?
>
> 32   He who did not spare His own Son, but delivered Him up for us all, how will He not also with Him freely give us all things?
>
> 33   Who will bring a charge against God's elect? God is the one who justifies;
>
> 34   who is the one who condemns? Christ Jesus is He who died, yes, rather who was raised, who is at the right hand of God, who also intercedes for us.
>
> 35   Who shall separate us from the love of Christ? Shall tribulation, or distress, or persecution, or famine, or nakedness, or peril, or sword?
>
> —Romans 8

For anyone to try to claim that the "elect" of God who are here on the earth during the tribulation are somehow Jews and not Christians is taking a great deal of liberty with the Scriptures. Jesus said that, "You have not chosen me, but I have chosen you..." (John 15:16, *KJV*). We are God's elect, and God's elect will be here during the tribulation, according to Jesus.

IS JESUS COMING WITH ANGELS OR WITH SAINTS?

When the Scriptures talk about Jesus coming down from heaven to the earth, He is coming with His angels. The angels then will gather up the Christians (the saints, the elect) and take them to Mount Zion. When He comes to Mount Zion, He comes with both the angels and the Old Testament saints and New Testament Christians.

Over and over again, Jesus Himself talked about returning to the earth with His angels:

27   "For the Son of Man is going to come in the glory of His Father with His angels; and WILL THEN RECOMPENSE EVERY MAN ACCORDING TO HIS DEEDS...."
—Matthew 16

31   "But when the Son of Man comes in His glory, and all the angels with Him, then He will sit on His glorious throne...."
—Matthew 25

38   "For whoever is ashamed of Me and My words in this adulterous and sinful generation, the Son of Man will also be ashamed of him when He comes in the glory of His Father with the holy angels."
—Mark 8

Paul understood this very clearly, as we can see in his letter to the church at Thessalonica:

7   and *to give* relief to you who are afflicted and to us as well when the Lord Jesus shall be revealed from heaven with His mighty angels in flaming fire,...
—2 Thessalonians 1

When Jesus gave His revelation and visions to John, He

showed him this in one of the visions that dealt explicitly with
His return:

> **11   And I saw heaven opened; and behold, a white
> horse, and He who sat upon it is called Faithful and
> True; and in righteousness He judges and wages war.**
>
> **12   And His eyes *are* a flame of fire, and upon His
> head *are* many diadems; and He has a name written
> *upon Him* which no one knows except Himself.**
>
> **13   And *He is* clothed with a robe dipped in blood;
> and His name is called The Word of God.**
>
> **14   And the armies which are in heaven, clothed in
> fine linen, white *and* clean, were following Him on
> white horses.**
>
> **15   And from His mouth comes a sharp sword, so
> that with it He may smite the nations; and He will rule
> them with a rod of iron; and He treads the wine press
> of the fierce wrath of God, the Almighty.**
>
> **16   And on His robe and on His thigh He has a name
> written, "KING OF KINGS, AND LORD OF LORDS."**
>
> **—Revelation 19**

This is a beautiful picture of the angelic armies following
Christ down to the earth. Verse 11 starts a brand new vision,
as we can tell when John said, "And I saw." This has no relation whatsoever to the vision he had in Revelation 19:1-10. People can get confused if they try to run these two separate visions
together. Thus, one could not use this particular vision to claim
that all the Christians were in heaven, from the rapture, and
they came back with Jesus. The only place that the Bible
implies that Christ comes with His saints (and I believe that is
to Mount Zion) is in 1 Thessalonians:

> **11   Now may our God and Father Himself and Jesus
> our Lord direct our way to you;**
>
> **12   and may the Lord cause you to increase and
> abound in love for one another, and for all men, just as
> we also *do* for you;**
>
> **13   so that He may establish your hearts unblamable
> in holiness before our God and Father at the coming of**

our Lord Jesus with all His saints....

—1 Thessalonians 3

16   For the Lord Himself will descend from heaven with a shout, with the voice of the archangel, and with the trumpet of God; and the dead in Christ shall rise first.

17   Then we who are alive and remain shall be caught up together with them in the clouds to meet the Lord in the air, and thus we shall always be with the Lord.

—1 Thessalonians 4

We can see that this is really talking about the rapture, when Jesus Christ comes and the Christians get their resurrected bodies and go with Him to the Mount Zion area, where they will spend the millennium ruling and reigning with Jesus.

SUMMARY AND CONCLUSION

I have dealt with the three passages and other considerations very briefly. If you wish to pursue the matter further, I would recommend reading the two books that I have referred to in this chapter.

Let me conclude by saying that the three passages that we have dealt with here at best might very *obliquely suggest* that there *might* be a rapture at the beginning of the tribulation. However, weighing this against the clear and explicit statements that we will be transformed at the last trumpet, that the resurrection in Revelation 20 is the first resurrection, and that Jesus will raise us up on the very last day of this age, leads me—based on the scriptural evidence—to conclude that the rapture will take place at the end of the tribulation.

I believe it is unwise to rest your future—and that of your loved ones—on the three passages discussed in this chapter, hoping they indicate that you will be "snatched away" and not go through the tribulation. I do not see the support in the Scriptures for such a position.

If someone were to err on this important subject, it would

be far better to err on the side of expecting to go through some troubled times than to expect to be exempted from the tribulation and find oneself in the middle of it. I could see that occurrence shaking someone's faith to the core: if one were taught to look for a pre-tribulation rapture and it didn't happen that way, that individual could well question the rest of what he had been taught about Jesus. It could be a source of great fear to find oneself in the middle of the tribulation, if all teaching had led one to believe he would not be there for those events.

WHY THE TIMING OF THE RAPTURE IS SIGNIFICANT TO YOU

In my early days as a Christian, I didn't view the timing of the rapture as an issue of importance. I figured our fellowship was around the person of Jesus and that was all that really mattered—not doctrinal issues.

I still believe that is true, but the Lord has shown me that what we believe about the timing of the rapture *is* much more important than I initially thought, as I said at the beginning of this book. It can make a tremendous difference in our day-to-day walk with the Lord and our daily decisions.

If someone believes he is going to be "snatched out" in a rapture before any real trouble hits the earth, it would be easy to slip into the attitude of, "I don't need to do anything—God will take care of me, regardless of what comes." It is true, God *is* our only source and true protection, but there may well be things that He wants to accomplish in our lives in preparation for what lies ahead. Too often, I have seen people hold the "pan-tribulation view" ("everything will pan out") as a cop-out to really seeking God on this matter.

On the other hand, if you believe that some really tough times are coming and you will go through them, there is a strong motivation to seek God diligently, to get familiar with the Scriptures and commit portions to memory, to become His bondslave, to learn to hear and obey His voice, and to make any preparations He may lead you to make. I believe that is why

God has called me to help awaken the body of Christ to prayer-fully reexamine what the Scriptures have to say on the subject.

We also need to examine the position historically held by the church concerning the timing of the rapture in relation to the coming great tribulation. What has the church believed during the centuries since the days of Jesus? Those who walked with Jesus must have had the correct information. What did they pass on to subsequent believers?

We will examine the answers to these questions in the next chapter.

9

THE HISTORIC POSITION OF THE CHURCH CONCERNING THE RAPTURE

Many Christians who have grown up in America in the last fifty years have never heard anything taught but a pre-tribulation rapture. Therefore, a post-tribulation rapture might sound like a new concept.

Actually the opposite is true. Through the centuries, the church has unanimously believed that Christians would go through the tribulation. The pre-tribulation view is a very new theory, only begun in 1830.

To give you a little background, we quote from Dr. Alexander Reese's book, *The Approaching Advent of Christ,* written in 1937. In it, he outlined the church's historic position on the rapture and the coming of Christ in power and glory. Here is this respected author and historian's summary of this subject:

"Until the second quarter of the nineteenth century general agreement existed among pre-millennial advocates of our Lord's Coming concerning the main outlines of the prophetic future: amidst differences of opinion on the interpretation of the Apocalypse and other portions of Scripture, the following scheme stood out as fairly representative of the school:

(1)   The approaching Advent of Christ to this world will be visible, personal, and glorious.

(2)   This Advent, though in itself a single crisis, will be accompanied and followed by a variety of phenomena bearing upon the history of the Church, of Israel, and the world. Believers who survive till the advent will be transfigured and translated to meet the approaching Lord, together with the saints raised and changed at the first resurrection. Immediately follow-

ing this, Antichrist and his allies will be slain, and Israel, the covenant people, will repent and be saved, by looking upon Him whom they pierced.

(3)   Thereupon the Messianic Kingdom of prophecy, which, as the Apocalypse informs us, will last for a thousand years, will be established in power and great glory in a transfigured world. The nations will turn to God, war and oppression cease, and righteousness and peace cover the earth.

(4)   At the conclusion of the kingly rule of Christ and His saints, the rest of the dead will be raised, the Last Judgment ensue, and a new and eternal world be created.

(5)   No distinction was made between the Coming of our Lord, and His Appearing, Revelation, and Day, because these were all held to be synonymous, or at least related, terms, signifying always the one Advent in glory at the beginning of the Messianic Kingdom.

(6)   Whilst the Coming of Christ, no matter how long the present dispensation may last, is the true and proper hope of the church in every generation, it is nevertheless conditioned by the prior fulfillment of certain signs or events in the history of the Kingdom of God: the Gospel has first to be preached to all nations; the Apostasy and the Man of Sin be revealed, and the Great Tribulation come to pass. Then shall the Lord come.

(7)   The Church of Christ will not be removed from the earth until the Advent of Christ at the very end of the present Age: the Rapture and the Appearing take place at the same crisis; hence Christians of that generation will be exposed to the final affliction under Antichrist.

Such is a fair statement of the fundamentals of Premillennialism as it has obtained since the close of the Apostolic Age. There have been differences of opinion on details and subsidiary points, but the main outline is as I have given it....

Yet the undeniable fact is that this "any-moment" view of Christ's Return only originated about 1830, when Darby gave forth at the same time the mistaken theory of the Secret Coming and Rapture; but all down the centuries there had existed Christians who longed for the Revelation of Christ, whilst expecting that Antichrist would come first....

All down the centuries the Church expected Christ's Coming after the arrival of Antichrist, according to the teaching of Christ and His Apostles. Only in 1830 did a school arise that treats with intolerance, and often with contempt, the attitude of those who had looked for Him in the manner just named. Not the slightest respect was paid to a view that had held the field for 1,800 years.

—Grand Rapids Intern. Publications,
Grand Rapids, MI, pp. 17, 18, 227, 240

HOW THE PRE-TRIBULATION
RAPTURE THEORY BEGAN

Dave MacPherson has done an excellent job researching the roots of the pre-tribulation rapture theory. If anyone wants to do detailed research on this subject, I would highly recommend his book, *The Incredible Cover-Up*. In Chapter 6 of his book, this is what MacPherson had to say:

In the summer of 1971 I was haunted by a certain question: who was the woman in Edward Irving's church who made that utterance some writers refer to, and what did she really say? A few books state that pre-trib rapture teaching began as a result of one woman's charismatic utterance, and it wasn't long before my journalistic curiosity was thoroughly aroused. I determined to search until I had found the answers—no matter how long it took....

On October 20, 1971, while rummaging through stacks of uncatalogued and not-for-sale books on Irvingism in the back of an Illinois bookstore, I discovered a rare copy of Norton's book and persuaded the owner to sell it to me.

Miss M. M., according to Norton's first chapter, was Margaret Macdonald of Port Glasgow, Scotland. Excitedly thumbing through the pages, I soon found what I was looking for:

Marvellous light was shed upon Scripture, and especially on the doctrine of the second Advent, by the revived spirit of prophecy. In the following account by Miss M. M—, of an evening during which the power of the Holy Ghost rested upon her for several successive hours, in mingled prophecy and vision, we have an instance; for here we first see the distinction between that final stage of the Lord's coming, when every eye shall see Him, and His prior appearing in glory to them that look for Him.

There are two astonishing admissions in this paragraph. Norton says Margaret MacDonald saw a two-stage coming, and that this was the *first* time such a distinction was made!

Immediately after this amazing paragraph are these words:

She writes:—"I felt this needed to be revealed, and that there was great great darkness and error about it; but suddenly what it was burst upon me with a glorious light."
—Omega Publications, P.O. Box 4130, Medford, OR 97501, pp. 36, 37

(For the actual copy of Margaret Macdonald's handwritten account of her vision, we would refer you to Appendix B.)

MACPHERSON'S SUMMARY

In Chapter 10 of *The Incredible Cover-up,* Dave MacPherson summarizes the origin of the pre-tribulation rapture theory this way:

We have seen that a young Scottish lassie named Margaret Macdonald had a private revelation in Port Glasgow, Scotland, in the early part of 1830 that a select group of Christians would be caught up to meet Christ in the air before the days of Antichrist. An eye-and-ear-witness, Robert Norton M.D., preserved her handwritten account of her pre-trib rapture revelation in two of his books, and said it was the first time anyone ever split the second coming into two distinct parts, or stages....

Margaret's views were well-known to those who visited her home, among them John Darby of the Brethren. Within a few months her distinctive prophetic outlook was mirrored in the September, 1830, issue of *The Morning Watch* and the early Brethren assembly at Plymouth, England. Early disciples of the pre-trib interpretation often called it a new doctrine. Setting dates for Christ's return was a common practice at that time....

Following my discovery of Norton's book in an Illinois bookstore in 1971, and before our trip to Great Britain, I corresponded with a number of top scholars, sharing excerpts from the book and asking their reactions. (These men are evangelical leaders and their names are as familiar to Christians as Coca-Cola is around the globe.)

A Missouri seminary president wrote back: "It really is a most interesting historical fact to observe that the pre-tribulation rapture originated in this astonishing way."

A professor in a Texas seminary said in a letter: "What is stated in Norton's book is new to me, and I am unable to evaluate it. My understanding was that, while Darby was the main spokesman for pre-tribulationism, there were many with whom he was associated that were studying together and developed this doctrine almost simultaneously."

An Oregon Bible teacher wrote: "You will be interested to know that many years ago I had dinner in Seattle with a then middle-aged couple who were members of the Catholic Apostolic Church (Irvingite sect). At that time I believed in pre-tribism and told them so. They asked me where I got the doctrine. I told them 'from the Bible.' They said, 'No, you didn't' and went on to tell me how it was not in the Bible but revealed to their church through one of their prophetesses around the middle of the 19th century."

A Kentucky seminary professor who is also a noted author said this in reply: "On biblical and historical grounds I had traced the idea of a pre-tribulation rapture to J.N. Darby about the year 1830, but I did not know about Margaret Macdonald. Thanks so very much for helping me on this point. It is good to have theological detectives of your type who will trace things down."

A Minnesota college professor and well-known authority on dispensational development wrote: "Let me say, first of all, that I should be most grateful to you if you would send me the complete photostat of Miss M. M.'s remarks. The photostat you sent ended at the bottom of page 15 of Norton's book before M. M. had actually said anything about the any-moment coming. The photographed passage contains only Norton's statement that Miss M. M. had revealed the doctrine of the two comings. I presume that she does say something more explicit in the following pages of her transcribed testimony. If she does, I would be most interested in seeing it. Whenever I have traced down references to the origin of the doctrine of the any-moment coming in an ecstatic utterance in Irving's church, I have run into this same problem. The utterance which is supposed to contain the revelation in fact contains nothing of substance. If Miss M. M.'s testimony does in fact contain a clear statement of the doctrine I would be most interested to see it." ...

These replies are representative of those from hundreds of scholars, and the really big surprise was to discover that the overwhelming majority of today's best-known evangelical scholars have rejected the idea of a secret two-stage rapture even though these same scholars have largely been in the dark about the origin of such teaching.

In the preceding pages are many references to speaking in unknown tongues. The evidence I have been privileged to find has shown that Margaret had her pre-trib revelation *before* she ever spoke with tongues; in fact, the tongues were a completely separate item (although some early pre-trib teachers were indeed tongues-speakers) and pre-trib rapture doctrine did not originate in an utterance of tongues, as some have charged. Margaret claimed her revelation was based only upon her study of Scripture passages.

Concerning charismatic gifts as they appear in various denominations today, since the overwhelming majority of present-day Bible scholars of note sees but a single unified coming of Christ for His church after the days of Antichrist, which are days "such as hath not been from the beginning of the world until now, no, nor ever shall be" (Matt. 24:21, ASV), it is possible that the Holy Spirit will empower the church during those days in ways we know little or nothing about right now.

In light of the evidence I have prayerfully and carefully given in this book relative to the pre-trib origin (which origin has been hidden for a long time), I would ask all Bible teachers to declare a moratorium on such teaching, at least until they can check this out for themselves.

This, then, is the true story of the unbelievable pre-trib origin.

—pp. 93-96

Margaret Macdonald had the initial vision, and then it was made popular at first by the Brethren, primarily through two ministers, Edward Irving and John Darby. However, all was not necessarily well in Irving's church, according to MacPherson.

Let's look now at another early writer who also made an important contribution—Robert Baxter of Doncaster, England. His book, *Narrative of Facts, Characterizing the Supernatural Manifestations in Members of Mr. Irving's Congregation, and Other Individuals in England and Scotland, and Formerly in the Writer Himself,* was published in 1833. Baxter had gone down to London in the fall of 1831, visited some of the prayer meetings which preceded the manifestation in Irving's church, and soon was a regular attendant at Irving's services. He then became endowed with the prophetic utterances and had a number of personal revelations. Later, when certain prophecies made by him and others simply were not fulfilled, he became disillusioned and felt that he had been deceived and had in turn deceived others.

—pp. 85-86

In addition, MacPherson makes this observation concerning Darby, in *The Incredible Cover-Up:*

One of the earliest Brethren leaders, Robert Gribble, described in Rowdon's *The Origins of the Brethren* p. 152, as one who "has been strangely neglected in most works on Brethren history," confessed in the early 1830s, after becoming acquainted with other Brethren, that he had adopted "a new view of unfulfilled prophecy" (Rowdon's book, p. 149) which included a pre-trib return of Christ. In an unguarded letter to a friend on July 24, 1834 (*Letter of J.N.D.*, pp. 25-26), Darby advocated a subtle introduction of the new pre-trib rapture view: "I think we ought to have something more of direct testimony as to the Lord's coming, and its bearing also on the state of the church: ordinarily, it would not be well to have it so clear, as it frightens people. We must pursue it steadily; it works like leaven, and its fruit is by no means seen yet; I do not mean leaven as ill, but the thoughts are new, and people's minds work on them, and all the old habits are against their feelings...." Note again Darby's admission that "the thoughts are new"—not "rediscovered!" Those who espouse the pre-trib view cannot name even one person from the time of Christ until 1830 who ever taught such a doctrine.

—p. 96

RESULTS OF THE
PRE-TRIBULATION RAPTURE THEORY

Dave MacPherson very accurately analyzes some of the sad results of Christians being lulled into believing the theory of the pre-tribulation rapture. He comments on this as follows:

The other day I opened up a newspaper with these alarming headlines:

MILLIONS MISSING AROUND WORLD
MASS KIDNAPPING
STOCK MARKET FACES CRASH
THOUSANDS ATTEMPT SUICIDE

The articles in the tabloid-size paper described scenes of horror and anguish around the globe—planes crashing, killer earthquakes, volcanoes erupting and tidal waves raging, teenage terror mobs roaming city streets, thousands of persons dying of heart attacks, and so on.

But my only response was a hearty chuckle. Why? Because this paper was merely another attempt to portray what many persons believe will happen when Christ returns for His church. They are the modern proponents of the pre-tribulation rapture, or pre-trib rapture—the sudden, unannounced happening that will cause the immediate disappearance of millions of true Christians from every nation. This same attitude is even expressed on bumper stickers like the one that warns: IF DRIVER DISAPPEARS, GRAB THE WHEEL.

We've already examined the bizarre origin of this doctrine and the apparent attempt to conceal it by J.N. Darby. Now I want to evaluate its widespread effects in western Christendom, especially in America. Beyond that I want to advocate a return to the more realistic post tribulational view, which was the only option within premillennialism prior to 1830 and which today is still the view held by the majority of premillennial Bible scholars. Christ's coming to receive His church and to judge the world will be one event, not two.

True, there are some scholars who affirm this but have not called themselves post-tribs, and in some cases their idea of the great tribulation has differed from the concepts of a seven or a three-and-a-half-year period.

But all have believed in a single coming of the Lord in the future, with the "catching up" of 1 Thessalonians 4 taking place after the days of Antichrist. Post-mills and a-mills, of course, hold to a single coming of Christ and most pre-mills, believe it or not, also see a one-stage advent that is necessarily post-tribulational.

There are at least two reasons why many Christians, especially here in America, are unaware that most of the top biblical scholars in the world today are post-tribs: (1) post-trib silence and (2) the vociferous dissemination of pre-trib ideas by their advocates.

The Silent Majority

George Ladd, a well-known post-trib pre-mill professor at Fuller Theological Seminary, stated in *The Blessed Hope*, p. 159, that those who see the church on earth during the days of Antichrist include a significant number of Christian leaders, but he added that they haven't been vocal, haven't wanted to be quoted, and haven't publicly declared their prophetic position.

One good reason for this silence is the fact that pre-trib dispensationalists have often used any and all means to squash their opposition....

The Pre-Trib Rapture view has caused the deaths of thousands of persons. Veteran missionary H. A. Baker shares his experiences of thirty-four years on the mission field in China in several of his books, including *Through Tribulation, Tribulation To Glory, Visions Beyond The Veil,* and *God in Ka Do Land.* He graphically points out the link between beliefs and actions.

Baker and other post-trib missionaries warned many Chinese Christians that Antichrist would come before Christ returns. Many heeded the warning and, before the Communist takeover, fled to the mountains where they have been able to continue witnessing for many years.

On the other hand, many pre-trib missionaries assured believers that they would be raptured away before any time of persecution—and history tells us that tens of thousands of Chinese Christians have been murdered since 1949!

In his book *Re-Entry*, p. 124, John Wesley White quotes *Times* magazine as reporting that tens of thousands of Christians are now languishing in prisons in China and Russia and other Communist countries. Those believers are, in some cases, undergoing torture, and their children are taken from them if they teach them about Christ.

Corrie ten Boom has also spoken of the Chinese Christians and their suffering: "the Christians were told that they didn't have to go through tribulation and we all know how it is in China." She added that all other Christians in free lands better be prepared for what is coming to them also. And in her article "The Coming Tribulation" in the Nov.-Dec., 1974 *Logos Journal* she wrote that those teaching "there will be no tribulation" and "the Christians will be able to escape all this" are really "the false teachers Jesus was warning us to expect in the latter days."

In *Sodom Had No Bible*, p.94, British evangelist Leonard Ravenhill also emphasizes that God didn't provide a rapture in 1940 for the Chinese Christians, nor for the believers in Hungary or in Russia.

"Demos Shakarian, director of the Full Gospel Businessmen, says that the Holy Spirit is now being poured out on believers to prepare them for rough times ahead. And Richard Wurmbrand told me that believers in Russia describe their existence these days as one of great tribulation and suffering. He added that America and other western countries will have the same thing one of these days. Larry Norman's song, "Right Here in America," also warns of persecution heading our way."

—pp. 101-104

In addition to the statements of the few men and women of God that Dave MacPherson mentions in the quote we just read, we could add the analysis of men like Dave Wilkerson in his recent book, *Set The Trumpet To Thy Mouth*. In it, Wilkerson warns Christians to get ready for tribulation, as he also did in his prior book, *The Vision*. Billy Graham's book, *'Til Armegeddon,* warns Christians to get ready to suffer until Armegeddon. Obviously, Billy Graham knows that Armegeddon happens at the end of the great tribulation.

We believe that those who are teaching the false theory of the pre-tribulation rapture are lulling Christians to sleep. They are telling them that they do not need to worry about anything, that all is going to go well and they will be raptured out before the tough times fall upon the earth.

What makes these teachers think that the Christians in America today are to be favored over the Christians who died in the Colosseum in Rome or the Soviet and Chinese Christians who were killed in this generation for their faith in Jesus Christ? Their cry is not a biblical one, but an emotional one. They cry, "God loves us too much to let us go through the tribulation." If that line of reasoning holds, then God would not have allowed the Christians in the first century to be eaten by lions, because He loved them so much. You cannot claim that He did not love the precious martyrs for Christ who have died in our own generation. There is no reason, other than wishful thinking, to believe that we will escape the persecution and tribulation that lie ahead simply because of God's love.

God does love us and He has provided a way that we can be protected through what is coming, but the choice is ours. We can decide to become His bondslave or not.

SUMMARY AND CONCLUSION

We have seen that the believers through the centuries uniformly and unanimously agreed that Christians would be raptured at the end of the great tribulation, at the time when Christ comes in power and glory. The pre-tribulation rapture theory is only of recent vintage, beginning in 1830 with a vision by Margaret Macdonald, a lady in Scotland. If you read Appendix B—her vision and Dave MacPherson's analysis of it—you can see that the vision could be called into serious question. Among other things, she believed that only a select group of believers would be raptured from the earth before the days of the antichrist, but she also saw other believers enduring the tribulation.

We believe it is time for the church to go back to the biblically-solid, historical position of believing that Christians will go through the tribulation, but that God will divinely protect His bondslaves from much that is coming upon the earth. A call is going out today to the body of Christ for Christians to become bondslaves, for Christians to join the end-time army of God that He is raising up, for Christians to become over-comers for Jesus Christ and for His glory.

Of course, if the tribulation is several hundred years away, then this is not of much concern to us. But, if indeed we are living in the end times of this age, and we are the generation that most likely will see Jesus Christ return to the earth, then the question of whether or not Christians will go through the tribulation is of vital importance.

So the next thing we need to do is to see what the likelihood is that we are the generation that will see this age come to an end.

10

THE FIG TREE AND ISRAEL

Before we look at whether or not we are living at the end of this age, we need to deal with a subject about which it is difficult for me to write. I believe that God would have me call attention to a false teaching that is commonly accepted as truth in the body of Christ, and to caution the teachers and authors who are propagating this teaching that enough is enough. It is not easy to come out strongly on this subject, but I must be true to what God calls me to do. I ask that you would be prayerful as you read this chapter, asking God to show you what He would wish to say to you personally and to the body of Christ. Also, please pray that He will protect you from misunderstanding my heart and motives, which are to help the body of Christ and to obey Him.

There are many Bible teachers, and especially those who teach about prophecy, who say that "God's prophetic clock started its countdown in 1948 when the nation of Israel was formed" and that Christ will return or the tribulation will start within one generation of that time. I say that that is nonsense. They base this on the teachings of Jesus in Matthew 24, wherein He gives a parable about a fig tree. They claim that this fig tree is the newly-formed nation of Israel. I feel that this is fantasy with no biblical basis.

According to most of these teachers, a generation is forty years. Thus, if you add forty years to 1948, then you have the tribulation beginning in 1988 and Christ's return in 1988, if you believe in a pre-tribulation rapture. In fact, there was a book written in the late 1970's entitled:

101 Reasons
Why Christ Will Return By 1988

This particular author was very explicit. However, most of the teachers and writers are less direct. They teach that Christ will return by 1988, without ever explicitly stating it. (If you are reading this after 1988 is over, parts of this chapter may be less relevant to you. However, I would encourage you to read it anyway so as not to miss the pertinent aspects of this discussion.)

Before we get into the biblical reasons why I disagree with these writers and teachers, we first need to look at what happened in 1981.

THE TRIBULATION DID NOT START IN 1981

The June 1980 issue of the Christian newsletter I edit, *End-Times News Digest* (*END*), had as the title of the main article:

"WILL THE TRIBULATION START IN 1981?"

The reason we discussed that subject in 1980, well ahead of time, was because many were teaching that the prophetic countdown clock started on May 14, 1948. Then if one added forty years to that, one would come up to 1988. If one then subtracted seven years for the tribulation, the great tribulation would therefore begin in 1981. Since all these people believed in a pre-tribulation rapture, in essence they were teaching that Christ would return in 1981.

Most of these teachers did not explicity state that that was what they were teaching, but that indeed was the essence of their teaching, as we outlined in the June 1980 issue of the newsletter.

In fact, Jeani and I went to hear a prominent Christian leader speak here in Medford on April 29 and 30, 1980. Accompanying us was a couple, the wife of which was the President of the Women's Aglow chapter. After hearing him talk on April 30, her comment was, "He is really teaching that Christ is coming back next year!" And we all agreed. The speaker did not state this in his talk, but this was the teaching that he gave. Much of the content of his talk is reproduced in that June 1980 issue of *End-Times News Digest*.

Also, in that issue, I quoted from a book written by another well-known pre-tribulationist, and it was evident that this was what he believed as well.

I wrote this issue early in 1980, so that if any of these teachers disagreed concerning my perception of what they were teaching, they had plenty of time to reply (and I would have been happy to have printed their response). However, none of them responded and then later in 1981, some began to deny that they ever taught that. They would sidestep the issue by saying, "I never said that Christ was going to return in 1981." That is true. They may never have said it explicitly; yet that is what they were teaching indirectly.

A wonderful Christian, who formerly attended a church in the Rogue Valley of Oregon, told me that in her church they were clearly teaching that Christ would return in 1981. However, after that year nothing was said about it and no admission of error was made.

Let me hasten to add that I love the brothers who believe in and teach the pre-tribulation rapture. They are my brothers in Christ and I praise the Lord for their ministries. I hope they reach more and more people for Jesus. However, I think that in some major areas of prophecy, they are misleading people. In 1981, they were able to soft-shoe dance their way around and start claiming that they were wrong in subtracting the seven years, and that the seven years would start in 1988.

In February of 1987, I wrote to these brothers with real love and concern, saying that if Christ does not return in 1988, they will have some public recanting to do. There is just so long that one can hold to an old theory after it has proven false. If the rapture does not occur in 1988, then either their teaching about the prophetic clock and Israel is wrong, or their pre-tribulation rapture theory is wrong, or both. Anyone who continues to listen to their teaching on prophecy after 1988 deserves the misleading that he will get, unless these brothers repent of error and turn to a more biblical position concerning the end times of the age.

WHERE DID THIS
1988 TEACHING GET ITS START?

The answer to the question of where this 1988 teaching got its start would require an entire book, to do it justice. Here we will just be able to look at it briefly. One of the key passages that we need to review in regard to this subject is in Matthew 24, a passage we discussed earlier in this book. To refresh your memory, Jesus and His disciples had just come from the temple and they were over on the Mount of Olives, where they frequently went. This beautiful hill overlooks the Temple Mount and, as they were sitting there, the disciples asked Christ the following:

> **3   And as He was sitting on the Mount of Olives, the disciples came to Him privately, saying, "Tell us, when will these things be, and what will be the sign of Your coming, and the end of the age?"**
> **—Matthew 24**

Evidently our Savior had taught them much about the age ending and about His return. Here they asked Him plainly what it was going to be like right before He came back and right before the age ended.

As we said in Chapter 1, the age that they are talking about is obviously the age that contained His return. They did not ask, "What will the end of the next age be like?" Therefore, the age that we are living in had already started there as they were sitting on the Mount of Olives.

As I said earlier, I do not know when it started, whether it was at Christ's conception, at His birth, when He was eight days old, when He was twelve, when He was baptized by John in the river Jordan, or at the Mount of Transfiguration. However, at some point in time, prior to this verse, the age that you and I are now living in had begun.

Since Jesus was going to be crucified in just a few days, I believe that He gave them a very straightforward answer to their question about what things would be like right before He came back and right before this age ended. Here is His answer:

4   And Jesus answered and said to them, "See to it that no one misleads you.

5   "For many will come in My name, saying, 'I am the Christ,' and will mislead many.

6   "And you will be hearing of wars and rumors of wars; see that you are not frightened, for *those things* must take place, but *that* is not yet the end.

7   "For nation will rise against nation, and kingdom against kingdom, and in various places there will be famines and earthquakes.

8   "But all these things are *merely* the beginning of birth pangs.

9   "Then they will deliver you to tribulation, and will kill you, and you will be hated by all nations on account of My name.

10   "And at that time many will fall away and will deliver up one another and hate one another.

11   "And many false prophets will arise, and will mislead many.

12   "And because lawlessness is increased, most people's love will grow cold.

13   "But the one who endures to the end, he shall be saved.

14   "And this gospel of the kingdom shall be preached in the whole world for a witness to all the nations, and then the end shall come.

15   "Therefore when you see the ABOMINATION OF DESOLATION which was spoken of through Daniel the prophet, standing in the holy place (let the reader understand),

16   then let those who are in Judea flee to the mountains;

17   let him who is on the housetop not go down to get the things out that are in his house;

18   and let him who is in the field not turn back to get his cloak.

19   "But woe to those who are with child and to those who nurse babes in those days!

> **20**   "But pray that your flight may not be in the win-
> ter, or on a Sabbath;
> **21**   for then there will be a great tribulation, such as
> has not occurred since the beginning of the world until
> now, nor ever shall...."
>
> **—Matthew 24**

As we discussed in Chapter 2, we see here that the great
tribulation begins in verse 21, but Jesus tells us that preceding
that will be a time that he calls the "time of birth pangs." In
the time of birth pangs, there will be wars, famine, earth
upheavals, persecution and the gospel will go to all nations.

Also, before the great tribulation begins, Jesus said there
would be the abomination of desolation standing in the holy
place. As we saw earlier, the word desolation means "uninhabited" (Isaiah 6:11, Jeremiah 33:10, Jeremiah 50:13). So something is going to happen in Jerusalem that is going to make it
uninhabited *before* the great tribulation begins.

To show you the inconsistency of some people who teach
on the end times, I have asked some of them if they believed
in the abomination of desolation, and their answer was,
"Definitely yes." I then asked them if they believed that Jerusalem was going to become uninhabited, and their answer was,
"Definitely no." I pointed out to them that they could not
believe both, because if you believe in the abomination of desolation, then you would have to believe that Jerusalem is going
to become uninhabited prior to the great tribulation.

But that is not the main issue. Let us return to the description that Jesus gave of the end of this age. As we noted, the great
tribulation begins in verse 21, and we read about it as follows:

> **21**   for then there will be a great tribulation, such as
> has not occurred since the beginning of the world until
> now, nor ever shall.
> **22**   "And unless those days had been cut short, no
> life would have been saved; but for the sake of the elect
> those days shall be cut short.
> **23**   "Then if anyone says to you, 'Behold, here is the
> Christ,' or 'There He *is*,' do not believe *him*.

24   "For false Christs and false prophets will arise and will show great signs and wonders, so as to mislead, if possible, even the elect.

25   "Behold, I have told you in advance.

26   "If therefore they say to you, 'Behold, He is in the wilderness,' do not go forth, or, 'Behold, He is in the inner rooms,' do not believe *them*.

27   "For just as the lightning comes from the east, and flashes even to the west, so shall the coming of the Son of Man be.

28   "Wherever the corpse is, there the vultures will gather.

29   "But immediately after the tribulation of these days THE SUN WILL BE DARKENED, AND THE MOON WILL NOT GIVE ITS LIGHT, AND THE STARS WILL FALL from the sky, and the powers of the heavens will be shaken,

30   and then the sign of the Son of Man will appear in the sky, and then all the tribes of the earth will mourn, and they will see the SON OF MAN COMING ON THE CLOUDS OF THE SKY with power and great glory.

31   "And He will send forth His angels with A GREAT TRUMPET and THEY WILL GATHER TOGETHER His elect from the four winds, from one end of the sky to the other...."

—Matthew 24

In this passage, we not only see the great tribulation, but also what is going to happen immediately after it. Immediately after the tribulation, the angels will go out to collect the alive Christians from the four winds and the dead Christians from one end of the sky to the other, as we discussed in Chapter 5. This is talking about the time of the rapture.

A CLOSE LOOK AT THE FIG TREE

Jesus continued with His answer to the disciples' question this way:

> **32** "Now learn the parable from the fig tree: when its branch has already become tender, and puts forth its leaves, you know that summer is near;
>
> **33** even so you too, when you see all these things, recognize that He is near, *right* at the door.
>
> **34** "Truly I say to you, this generation will not pass away until all these things take place...."
>
> —Matthew 24

Jesus says here that we should take a lesson from nature: when we see a tree—in this case He used a fig tree—and its branch becomes tender and it puts forth leaves, we should know that it is spring and that summer is coming. Jesus then points out that when we begin to see all the things happen that He talked about in the early part of the chapter, we should recognize that Jesus is right at the door. Then He says that the generation that sees these things begin to happen will not pass away until *all* of the things that He mentioned in verses 4 through 31 take place.

His mentioning of the fig tree example had absolutely nothing to do with the Hebrews forming a nation. Jesus simply and plainly taught that the generation that began to see the earth upheavals, the famines and so forth was going to be the generation that would see His return, and that that generation would see all of the things that He had mentioned from verses 4 through 31.

There is no biblical evidence that Christ intended the fig tree mentioned here to be anything but simply a fig tree. There are those who try to make out the fig tree to represent Israel. I see no justification for arbitrarily applying the Matthew 24 passage about the fig tree to Israel and not this one, for example:

> **12** And on the next day, when they had departed from Bethany, He became hungry.
>
> **13** And seeing at a distance a fig tree in leaf, He went *to see* if perhaps He would find anything on it; and when He came to it, He found nothing but leaves, for it was not the season for figs....

20   And as they were passing by in the morning, they
saw the fig tree withered from the roots *up.*
21   And being reminded, Peter said to Him, "Rabbi,
behold the fig tree which You cursed has withered."
—Mark 11

If you ask proponents of the fig tree theory if this fig tree,
that Jesus cursed and caused to dry up and die, represents Israel,
they would say, "Absolutely not." I would encourage them to
be consistent in handling the Scriptures. I try to be consistent
but obviously do not always make it. However, when someone points out an inconsistency in something I have been
teaching, I try to correct it and acknowledge it publicly.

I cannot find a single Scripture that equates the nation of
Israel to a fig tree. I will give you some of the key verses that
these people use to try to come up with this:

7   Now when they told Jotham, he went and stood
on the top of Mount Gerizim, and lifted his voice and
called out. Thus he said to them, "Listen to me, O men
of Shechem, that God may listen to you.
8   "Once the trees went forth to anoint a king over
them, and they said to the olive tree, 'Reign over us!'
9   "But the olive tree said to them, 'Shall I leave my
fatness with which God and men are honored, and go
to wave over the trees?
10   "Then the trees said to the fig tree, 'You come,
reign over us!'
11   "But the fig tree said to them, 'Shall I leave my
sweetness and my good fruit, and go to wave over the
trees?'
12   "Then the trees said to the vine, 'You come, reign
over us!'
13   "But the vine said to them, 'Shall I leave my new
wine, which cheers God and men, and go to wave over
the trees?'
14   "Finally all the trees said to the bramble, 'You
come, reign over us!'
15   "And the bramble said to the trees, 'If in truth you
are anointing me as king over you, come and take ref-

uge in my shade; but if not, may fire come out from the bramble and consume the cedars of Lebanon.'..."

—Judges 9

There is nothing here in Judges 9 that equates Israel to the fig tree. Another Scripture that some teachers try to use is found in Deuteronomy:

7   "For the Lord your God is bringing you into a good land, a land of brooks of water, of fountains and springs, flowing forth in valleys and hills;

8   a land of wheat and barley, of vines and fig trees and pomegranates, a land of olive oil and honey;..."

—Deuteronomy 8

Here again, there is no way you can stretch that to say that Israel is represented by a fig tree. You could just as well say that pomegranates or barley represent Israel.

I have checked out all of the Scriptures that I can find concerning the fig tree and nowhere does it represent Israel. I would have to say that the statement of many of these people that: "Israel is always represented by the fig tree in the Scriptures" is simply a false statement.

I would welcome anyone to show me from the Scriptures where the nation of Israel is ever described as a fig tree. In Jeremiah 24:5, some of the Jews were compared to figs, and in Hosea 9:10, some of the fathers were compared to the first fruit on a fig tree, but I cannot find anywhere in the Scriptures that the nation of Israel is called a fig tree. I would appreciate being enlightened on the subject. I am open to learning.

A tree that does represent Israel, at least in one instance in the Scriptures, is the olive tree. You can read Romans 11:17-24 and see this very clearly.

If we examine Luke 21, which is a parallel passage to Matthew 24, we see even more clearly that the fig tree does not represent Israel in Christ's Olivet discourse. This is a long passage, but please read it carefully.

5   And while some were talking about the temple, that it was adorned with beautiful stones and votive gifts, He said,

6   *"As for* these things which you are looking at, the days will come in which there will not be left one stone upon another which will not be torn down."

7   And they questioned Him, saying, "Teacher, when therefore will these things be? And what *will be* the sign when these things are about to take place?"

8   And He said, "See to it that you be not misled; for many will come in My name, saying, 'I am *He*,' and, 'The time is at hand'; do not go after them.

9   And when you hear of wars and disturbances, do not be terrified; for these things must take place first, but the end *does* not *follow* immediately."

10   Then He continued by saying to them, "Nation will rise against nation, and kingdom against kingdom,

11   and there will be great earthquakes, and in various places plagues and famines; and there will be terrors and great signs from heaven.

12   "But before all these things, they will lay their hands on you and will persecute you, delivering you to the synagogues and prisons, bringing you before kings and governors for My name's sake.

13   "It will lead to an opportunity for your testimony.

14   "So make up your minds not to prepare beforehand to defend yourselves;

15   for I will give you utterance and wisdom which none of your opponents will be able to resist or refute.

16   "But you will be delivered up even by parents and brothers and relatives and friends, and they will put *some* of you to death,

17   and you will be hated by all on account of My name.

18   "Yet not a hair of your head will perish.

19   "By your endurance you will gain your lives.

20   "But when you see Jerusalem surrounded by armies, then recognize that her desolation is at hand.

21   "Then let those who are in Judea flee to the mountains, and let those who are in the midst of the city depart, and let not those who are in the country enter the city;

22   because these are days of vengeance, in order that all things which are written may be fulfilled.

23   "Woe to those who are with child and to those who nurse babes in those days; for there will be great distress upon the land, and wrath to this people,

24   and they will fall by the edge of the sword, and will be led captive into all the nations; and Jerusalem will be trampled under foot by the Gentiles until the times of the Gentiles be fulfilled.

25   "And there will be signs in sun and moon and stars, and upon the earth dismay among nations, in perplexity at the roaring of the sea and the waves,

26   men fainting from fear and the expectation of the things which are coming upon the world; for the powers of the heavens will be shaken.

27   "And then they will see THE SON OF MAN COMING IN A CLOUD with power and great glory...."

Luke 21

One thing to note from this passage (verse 20) is that in the end times of this age, Jerusalem will be surrounded by armies. At that point, she is about to become uninhabited ("her desolation is at hand").

As Christ's conclusion to His teaching about the end of the age, He shares this parable:

28   "But when these things begin to take place, straighten up and lift up your heads, because your redemption is drawing near."

29   And He told them a parable: "Behold the fig tree and all the trees;

30   as soon as they put forth leaves, you see it and know for yourselves that summer is now near.

31   "Even so you, too, when you see these things happening, recognize that the kingdom of God is near.

32   "Truly I say to you, this generation will not pass away until all things take place...."

—Luke 21

We see in verse 29 that when the fig tree *and all the other trees* put forth leaves, we know that summer is near. Thus, obviously this illustration has nothing to do with establishing a

Hebrew nation. Jesus is simply taking an example out of nature about all the trees putting forth their leaves as a signal that summer is near. If the fig tree represents the nation of Israel being formed in 1948, what do all of the other trees represent? The answer is that they are not meant to represent anything but trees, and neither is the fig tree.

In the same way, Jesus tells us that when we see the things beginning to happen that He described earlier in the chapter, then we know that if we are that generation, within the length of that generation all of it will completely happen. This includes His return in power and glory to rule and reign on the earth for a thousand years! Even so, come King Jesus!

A QUICK REVIEW

So let us review what we have covered in this chapter. We see that the fig tree does not represent Israel in the first place, but if it did, we would also have to take into account passages such as the one in which Christ cursed the fig tree and caused it to die.

We have also seen that Christ was not talking about a fig tree being "planted," such as those would imply who teach the 1948-prophetic-clock theory, which is obviously false. Christ taught a simple parable from nature about an existing fig tree and other trees that were already planted and were in place. He simply said that when you see them put out leaves, you know it is spring. And just as surely, when you see the things begin to happen that are in the time of birth pangs, then you know that Jesus is at the door and that the generation that sees these things will see His return.

Isn't it exciting that most likely we are the generation which is going to see all these things begin to happen and come to full fruition with the return of our glorious Savior, Jesus Christ, here on the earth? How I am looking forward to His return! I love Him so!

BEWARE OF FALSE TEACHINGS

You notice that I said, "Beware of false teachings," not "Beware of false teachers." There are many good Christian brothers who teach that the fig tree is the nation of Israel; I believe they are wrong on that particular subject, but much of what they teach about Jesus is really good and really glorifies Jesus Christ. Therefore, I would not classify them as false teachers. They are precious brothers of mine in Jesus Christ. As a watchman, however, I would encourage you to stop listening to them on things concerning prophecy, unless they turn from these false teachings.

It is becoming critical that you weigh very carefully everything that you are taught to be sure that it matches with the Scriptures. If someone tells you, "Israel is always referred to as a fig tree," then you are going to need to take your concordance and look up under "fig" to see if this is so. If it is not so, that gives you reason to discard that teaching and certainly to be more cautious regarding other things that particular teacher might proclaim to you.

There are many false teachings about the end times of this age that are going around today. Another one of them is that the Gog-Magog war might happen at any time. That, too, is not scriptural. I deal with this in depth in the book, *The Coming Climax of History.* In it, we solidly back up by Scripture everything that we say. However, with my writings and teachings also, you still must be sure yourself that they match the Scriptures. I encourage you to check them out.

In that book, I also deal with the all-important subject of understanding who Israel is today, a key to understanding biblical prophecy. In addition, there is an in-depth discussion of the various wars and battles that go on in the end times. (If these subjects are of interest to you, you may use the form at the end of this book to send for information on how to order a copy of *The Coming Climax of History.*)

WHY ARE THESE THINGS IMPORTANT?

Some people think that we should only concentrate on becoming like Jesus and witnessing and not on things concerning the end of this age. It is interesting that one-third of the Bible is prophecy. If we disregard it, are we not really saying that God made a mistake by including that one-third of the Bible? God put it there for a reason and the reason is for us to read it and understand it.

In the end of this age, many Christians are going to be misled and deceived. Remember—we read this in Matthew 24:

11 "And many false prophets will arise, and will mislead many...."

Here Christ is talking about many Christians being misled at the end of this age. This misleading can go a long way to damaging their faith.

For example, when Jerusalem is surrounded by armies and then some abomination in it causes Jerusalem to become uninhabited, some Christians are likely to lose faith in God, because they are convinced that God would never let down the nation of Israel.

In order that things like that do not shake your faith, you need to know clearly what the Bible has to say about the end of this age. I do not want your faith to be shaken. I want you to know the truth. Among other things, the truth will set you free from fear. It will set you free from fear of the future and the unknown.

Lest you misunderstand, let me clarify one thing: I love the nation of Israel. I have visited there and conducted a tour there, which was wonderful. They are an incredible people, with a marvelous heritage, and the U.S. and other free countries need to support them more than we do. But that has nothing to do with our discussion here of whether the forming of that nation in 1948 is a date by which we can judge when Christ will return.

WE MUST BE WILLING TO CHANGE

Perhaps in the past you have believed that the prophetic clock started in 1948 with the establishment of the nation, Israel; that the nation of Israel was the fig tree; and that forty years after her establishment this whole thing would wrap up. Maybe you have even taught this to others.

If the tribulation does not begin in 1988 (and, therefore—for those who believe in a pre-tribulation rapture—Christ's return does not come in 1988), by January 1, 1989, this chapter should challenge you then to recant of a false teaching and declare God's truth. The quicker you let go of the old, when God shows you that you are in error, and embrace what He shows you is truth, the more He can use you.

Just as an example, I used to believe that the rapture would occur before the tribulation, because that was what I had been taught. But when God showed me otherwise, from the Scriptures and the counsel of a brother in Christ, I did not hang on to what I had previously believed but gladly changed. I also once believed that the fig tree was Israel, because that was what I had heard others say. Then I checked it out in the Scriptures for myself, asking the Holy Spirit to teach me, and I learned that there was no basis for that belief.

Therefore I cannot fault someone who believes that way today. The difficulty comes if one refuses to check the Scriptures and/or change.

There may be many Christians reading this book of varied persuasions—pastors, authors, teachers, and laymen alike—who need to make an examination of the Scriptures, asking the Holy Spirit to teach them the truth concerning some of these subjects raised herein, regardless of what their prior beliefs might have been. Then if the Lord shows them something different, they need to have the courage (guts) to acknowledge it. If we are "truth seekers," this should be a joy for us and not something to be dreaded.

Jim Hylton recently said:

"There are no graduates from the school of Christ. No alumni are listed as achievers who have gone out to make their mark on the world. What would approach graduation is not going out from Christ but going to be with Him in heaven. Marks are made by those who talk with Him. Those who make such marks are not graduates but students who are learning. Leaders are disciples. Unlike so-called old soldiers, who never die but just fade away, old disciples never die or fade away. Old disciples go on learning."

—Pastor of Lake County Baptist Church,
Ft. Worth, Texas

Hopefully, our discussion in this chapter of this wide-spread false teaching concerning the end of this age will serve to encourage you to do your own study, in order to verify the truth of what you are being taught. If it has done that, you are the richer for it.

We can now move on to examine the likelihood of our being the generation of the fig tree—that is, the generation that will see Jesus Christ return.

11

ARE WE LIVING
IN THE END TIMES?

Before we can intelligently discuss whether or not we are living in the end times, we must understand what is meant by the "end times."

This is a fairly loose term, probably with many definitions. Most often it is used in Christian circles to indicate the period of time at the end of this age, which would include the time immediately preceding and including the tribulation. This is the way we will be using the term in this book. Some people might incorrectly interpret it as the time of the end of the world.

The phrase "end times" is a fairly common one, although it is not specifically found in the Scriptures. The Bible does refer to "the end" and "the end of the age" in a number of verses. You may recall our discussion of "ages" in Chapter 1. In light of that, a more descriptive term for the "end times" would be the "end times of this present age." A term that is found in the Scriptures is the "last days." More precisely, this would be the "last days of this present age." This would be the period of time preceding the last day of this age, much as the last minutes of a football game precede the last minute of the game.

WHAT WILL HAPPEN DURING THE
LAST DAYS OF THIS PRESENT AGE?

We have some clues from various places in the Scriptures as to what will occur during the "last days" of this present age. In writing to the Christians who were scattered throughout the world, Peter gives this insight into what it will be like in the last days:

> **3 Know this first of all, that in the last days
> mockers will come with their mocking, following after
> *their* own lusts,**
> **4   and saying, "Where is the promise of His com-
> ing? For *ever* since the fathers fell asleep, all continues
> just as it was from the beginning of creation."**
> **—2 Peter 3**

We see that there will be mockers making fun of Christianity and of God. They will probably even claim something
ridiculous like "God is dead."

In writing to his spiritual son, Timothy, Paul gives us a
different viewpoint on the difficult times that will be coming
in the last days in a passage we quoted earlier, in Chapter 2.
He depicts mankind as becoming very self-centered, unholy
and treacherous. He says that men will love pleasure more than
they love God, even though they might have a form of
"religion."

> **1   But realize this, that in the last days difficult
> times will come.**
> **2   For men will be lovers of self, lovers of money,
> boastful, arrogant, revilers, disobedient to parents,
> ungrateful, unholy,**
> **3   unloving, irreconcilable, malicious gossips,
> without self-control, brutal, haters of good,**
> **4   treacherous, reckless, conceited, lovers of pleas-
> ure rather than lovers of God;**
> **5   holding to a form of godliness, although they
> have denied its power; and avoid such men as these.**
> **6   For among them are those who enter into house-
> holds and captivate weak women weighed down with
> sins, led on by various impulses,**
> **7   always learning and never able to come to the
> knowledge of truth.**
> **—2 Timothy 3**

As we look at this passage of Scripture, we get some additional hints as to what the last days will be like. I believe that

we are seeing this occurring now. Surely men are lovers of self, lovers of money, disobedient to parents, and lovers of pleasure rather than lovers of God. You will have to decide for yourself whether or not you think that our present time qualifies in meeting the criteria laid down in these verses. I know that with God as your guide you will be able to discern whether or not it applies to today.

Another passage that gives insight into the last days is found in Acts 2, where Peter quotes from the prophet Joel:

15 "For these men are not drunk, as you suppose, for it is *only* the third hour of the day;
16 but this is what was spoken of through the prophet Joel:
17 'AND IT SHALL BE IN THE LAST DAYS,'
    GOD SAYS,
    'THAT I WILL POUR FORTH OF MY
    SPIRIT UPON ALL MANKIND;
    AND YOUR SONS AND YOUR DAUGHTERS
    SHALL PROPHESY,
    AND YOUR YOUNG MEN SHALL SEE
    VISIONS,
    AND YOUR OLD MEN SHALL DREAM
    DREAMS;
18 EVEN UPON MY BONDSLAVES, BOTH MEN
    AND WOMEN,
    1 WILL IN THOSE DAYS POUR FORTH
    OF MY SPIRIT
    And they shall prophesy.
19 'AND I WILL GRANT WONDERS IN THE
    SKY ABOVE,
    AND SIGNS ON THE EARTH BENEATH,
    BLOOD AND FIRE, AND VAPOR OF SMOKE.
20 'THE SUN SHALL BE TURNED INTO
    DARKNESS
    AND THE MOON INTO BLOOD,
    BEFORE THE GREAT AND GLORIOUS
    DAY OF THE LORD SHALL COME.
21 'AND IT SHALL BE, THAT EVERY ONE

**WHO CALLS ON THE NAME OF THE
LORD SHALL BE SAVED.'..."**

—Acts 2

We see here that the Holy Spirit will be poured out on Christians during the last days. The young will prophesy and have visions, and God will speak to the old men in dreams. I believe that this is being fulfilled. The gifts of prophecy and visions have been poured out by the Holy Spirit upon true believers in Christ, Prostestant and Catholic alike. I have personal knowledge that God is speaking to old men in dreams.

I believe that the signs in the sky mentioned in verses 19 and 20 will be part of the tribulation, for these are almost the exact words used by John in describing some of the coming catastrophes. All this will precede the great and glorious day of the Lord's return, according to verse 20.

THE DAY OF THE LORD

Since the preceding passage from Acts refers to the day of the Lord, we might just comment on that subject very briefly. If you ask most people—even teachers on prophecy—what the day of the Lord is, they tend to think that it might be the tribulation, or at least that the tribulation is the first part of the day of the Lord.

For example, in his book, *Dispensational Truth*, Dr. Clarence Larkin says this:

> "The day of the Lord, that is, the day of vengeance of our Lord, includes the period of the great tribulation and the millennium that follows."

—Rev. Clarence Larkin Estate,
Glenside, PA 19038, p. 53

I was a bit unclear on this subject and a traveling Methodist Evangelist, Royal Edwards, who has an excellent slide show on end-times events, helped shed some light on this for me.

The Lord showed me that the day of the Lord follows the tribulation. This can be seen clearly in verse 20 of Acts 2 that we just read, wherein Peter is quoting from Joel 2:31. In it, we can clearly see that the celestial signs—the sun being turned into darkness and the moon into blood—come *before* the day of the Lord:

> **31 The sun will be turned into darkness,**
> **And the moon into blood,**
> **Before the great and awesome day of the**
> **LORD comes.**
>
> **—Joel 2**

On the other hand, in talking about these same celestial signs, Jesus puts them *after* the great tribulation:

> **29 "But immediately after the tribulation of those days THE SUN WILL BE DARKENED, AND THE MOON WILL NOT GIVE ITS LIGHT, AND THE STARS WILL FALL from the sky, and the powers of the heavens will be shaken,**
> **30 and then the sign of the Son of Man will appear in the sky, and then all the tribes of the earth will mourn, and they will see the SON OF MAN COMING ON THE CLOUDS OF THE SKY with power and great glory.**
>
> **—Matthew 24**

We also know that when Jesus Christ comes back, among other things, He is coming back for judgment:

> **31 "But when the Son of Man comes in His glory, and all the angels with Him, then He will sit on His glorious throne.**
> **32 "And all the nations will be gathered before Him; and He will separate them from one another, as the shepherd separates the sheep from the goats;**
> **33 and He will put the sheep on His right, and the goats on the left...."**
>
> **—Matthew 25**

The Bible lets us know that the celestial signs and judgment both will be part of the day of the Lord:

> **9 Behold, the day of the LORD is coming,**
> **Cruel, with fury and burning anger,**

> To make the land a desolation;
> And He will exterminate its sinners
>   from it.
> 10 For the stars of heaven and their
>   constellations
>   Will not flash forth their light;
>   The sun will be dark when it rises,
>   And the moon will not shed its light.
> 11 Thus I will punish the world for its evil,
>   And the wicked for their iniquity;
> 12 I will make mortal man scarcer than
>   pure gold,
>   And mankind than the gold of Ophir.
> 13 Therefore I shall make the heavens
>   tremble,
>   And the earth will be shaken from its
>   place
>   At the fury of the LORD of hosts
>   In the day of His burning anger.
>   —Isaiah 13

An in-depth study on the day of the Lord will reveal much more on this, but that is not the major issue here. We need to understand that the great tribulation *precedes* the day of the Lord, even though some people teach the contrary.

We all are going to experience the day of the Lord because, even if we die before Christ returns, we will be resurrected, if we are Christians, to stand before the judgment seat of Christ, which is the first event of the millennium. Most likely, we will experience the great tribulation, if we do not go to be with the Lord beforehand. However, as we are discussing in this chapter, there is an expanding awareness that we are living in the end of times of this age.

A GROWING WORLDWIDE AWARENESS

I travel all over the world and minister in other countries. Everywhere I go—Japan, Korea, Hong Kong, Malaysia, the Philippines, Indonesia, Europe, Latin America, Canada, South Africa, and the United States—the feeling is stronger and stronger among Christians that we are indeed living in the last days of this present age (the end times). Assuming that this prompting is of the Holy Spirit—and I have no reason to doubt that it is—it appears as though God is speaking to the hearts of Christians, independent of one another, telling us to ready ourselves, for we are living during the time of the end of this age. This worldwide feeling that we are living in the end times is shared by pre-, mid- and post-tribulationists alike, and it is something that no human being or organization could achieve.

In recent years, if you were to go to a local Christian bookstore to find out what our Christian writers were saying, these are some of the titles that you would have found on the shelves:

The End of This Present World
The Tribulation People
There's a New World Coming
Armageddon
The End of the Days
Goodbye World
How to Recognize the Antichrist
The Terminal Generation
The Antichrist is Alive Today
Those Who Remain
The Late Great Planet Earth
World War III and the Destiny of America
Get All Excited—Jesus is Coming Soon
The Soon to be Revealed Antichrist
Moments to Go
Jesus is Coming—Get Ready Christian

The titles themselves tell you a great deal about what these Christian leaders and authors are sensing in the Spirit. Almost every one of them either states or implies in his writing that he feels Jesus is coming soon, and that we are living in the end times. (Some of them feel that the rapture will occur at the beginning of the tribulation. Our concern here is awareness of Christian laymen, leaders, and writers that we are likely living in the last days of this present age.)

It is interesting to note what a couple of these authors have to say. Dr. Charles R. Taylor says this in his book, *Those Who Remain:*

> The many documentations in this book give solid evidence that the rapture of the Church and God's judgment on Earth are both very, very near.
>
> The Lord has given us many prophecies about the signs of the times and His return. Now, those prophecies are coming to pass, and His return is not only imminent: It is at the very doors."
>
> —Today in Bible Prophecy, Inc., p. 11

Dr. Taylor feels very strongly that we are living in the end times, and that the antichrist is alive today. He even goes into detail as to who he believes to be the two most likely candidates for the antichrist.

The title of Hal Lindsey's book, *The Terminal Generation,* lets you know immediately that he feels this is the last or terminal generation of the present age. He says this:

> More and more people are becoming interested in Bible prophecy, not just as a whim, but as a verification of events in the world today. Scientists, psychologists, sociologists, and educators who might not believe in the Bible as the source of truth, are making the same predictions as those of the ancient prophets!
>
> We have seen significant changes on the world scene, even in the past five years: Arab power; Israel's deteriorating position; alignment of the Third World with the Arabs; an avalanche of crime and lawlessness; China's attempt to unify Asian countries behind it; famine, earthquakes, weapons of war; move toward one-worldism; decline of morality; increase in the occult.
>
> As an individual looks for a way to cope with life—as he searches for hope in what appears to be a hopeless world—many are helpless. In this state, there are many false hopes and false prophets waiting to occupy the void in empty lives.
>
> How discerning we must be! As Jesus has warned, "For false Christs and false prophets will arise and will show great signs and wonders, so as to mislead, if possible, even the elect" (Matthew 24:24).
>
> How alert we should be! When I see all these events com-

ing together simultaneously I feel like shouting, "Wake up, World, Jesus is almost here!

—Fleming H. Revell Company, p. 65

Both Dr. Taylor and Hal Lindsey feel that the nation of Israel is God's time clock. By reading correctly what is happening to Israel, some feel we can discern God's timetable for the last days. I do not agree with that but, according to these men, the clock started its final countdown in 1948 when Israel became a nation again. Some feel that there is absolutely no doubt that we are living in the last generation and that we will see Christ come back. I believe we can claim that the Spirit is saying we are living in the last generation, and that there is a high probability Christ will be coming back in our time, but there is no way we can be absolutely sure. We will examine my reasons for saying this, later in this chapter. However, let me hasten to add that, in looking at the Scriptures and the evidence in events of the world around us, it does appear as though the history of this present age is racing to a climax.

EVIDENCE OF THE LAST DAYS

One evidence that we are indeed living in the last days is that the Bible prophesies that in the last days major wars will be fought in the Mideast. Many years ago it was difficult to understand why this would be so. There was nothing over there but sand, desert and a few palm trees. But now one of the reasons is apparent to all: OIL. It is very clear how important and crucial that area is, since the vast majority of the world's oil reserves are in the Middle East.

A graph of the projected oil production of the world projected that world oil production will peak at about the year 1995, and by 2015 it will be only 50 percent of what it was at the peak. Thus, if there is going to be a major battle in the Mideast over oil, it certainly will occur somewhere between now and the beginning years of the next century.

An additional important factor for a major conflict in the Mideast is the rising to world power of both the U.S.S.R. and

China. Revelation 16 talks about the kings of the East and the armies that poured across the dried up Euphrates, which could well mean China. In fact, it even refers to this army from the East, in an indirect manner, as the "dragon." We see both the Soviets and China arming heavily militarily; certainly they would be able to engage in such conflicts.

Another thing that we see in the end times is the rise of a world government and a world dictator. At the turn of the century, it would have been almost impossible to have had a world dictator and a world government, since radio and television were not in any type of widespread use and computers had not yet been invented. All of this communication and computer equipment would be necessary for a world government and world economic system to function. It would have been technically difficult for some of the prophecies in Revelation to have been fulfilled in the early 1900's—such as the one that no man will be able to buy or sell without the mark of the beast, for example. Today with credit cards and computers, this type of control is technically within the realm of possibility.

Also, at the beginning of the century there was no need for a world government. Each country was independent, and the world monetary system was based on gold and was quite stable. After the United States went off of the gold standard in 1972, the currencies of the different nations began to float against each other. Today the world monetary system is in total chaos. As it continues to degenerate, there will be a demand for a new world economic system. This, of course, would have to be administered by something akin to a world government.

Another way to view this is that in the United States, from every side, there is a cry for a redistribution of wealth. The poor want it, many ministers want it, and the senators and congressmen evidently want it also. This redistribution is working because U.S. citizens, both rich and poor, are under the authority of the federal government. The government can therefore take from the rich (and middle class) and give to the poor.

In a similar way, there is a worldwide cry for redistribution of wealth from the richer nations to the poorer nations.

We see this in the Arab oil cartel. The Arabs are saying that they want a bigger slice of the world's pie. Many developing nations are saying the same thing and are borrowing money from the richer nations that they never intend to repay. If these poorer nations are to get wealth, it has to come from the richer nations. There are three basic ways that this transfer of wealth can occur:

1.   The richer nations can voluntarily give to the poorer nations.

2.   There can be war, wherein the poorer nations take from the richer nations.

3.   There can be a world government, which will have authority over all of the national governments. This world government will then have the power to take from the richer nations and give to the poorer nations.

I believe that the ultimate resolution of this problem will be the third option—a world government. There is pressure for this from almost every direction.

Along with the world government, we see in the Scriptures that in the end times there will be a world church, so to speak (the "prophet beast" in Revelation 13 will cause all the earth to worship the "dictator beast"). Again, at the beginning of this century, a world church would have seemed almost ridiculous. Today the World Council of Churches and the Catholics are moving progressively closer to one. Within a few years we could see a world church.

I could go on and on with the evidences of the events occurring today that match with prophecies. Yet I hesitate to do so, because in my lifetime I have seen Hitler, Mussolini, Stalin and even Henry Kissinger labeled as the antichrist. It is a bit dangerous to try to take a contemporary individual, nation or event and tack it solidly to a piece of prophecy. However, some of the worldwide movements—such as one toward a world government, a world church, and a world economic system— and the importance of the Middle East, are things that have never occurred before in the history of the world and could well be some of the beginning events of the last days.

THE END OF THE AGE—WHEN?

You may have some questions by now. The disciples did. I would like to go back to some Scriptures that we discussed earlier. In this first one, the disciples came to Jesus and asked Him perhaps one of the very questions that you have on your heart.

> **3   And as He was sitting on the Mount of Olives, the disciples came to Him privately, saying, "Tell us, when will these things be and what *will be* the sign of Your coming, and of the end of the age?"**
>
> **—Matthew 24**

You can see here that they asked Him plainly what the sign of His coming and of the end of the age would be. The rest of Chapter 24 is His answer to that question. We covered much of Matthew 24 in Chapter 2, but I would suggest that you take your own Bible and reread all of Christ's answer.

As to when these events would take place, Christ had this to say:

> **29   "But immediately after the tribulation of those days THE SUN WILL BE DARKENED, AND THE MOON WILL NOT GIVE ITS LIGHT, AND THE STARS WILL FALL from the sky, and the powers of the heavens will be shaken,**
> **30   and then the sign of the Son of Man will appear in the sky, and then all the tribes of the earth will mourn, and they will see the SON OF MAN COMING ON THE CLOUDS OF THE SKY with power and great glory.**
> **31   "And He will send forth His angels with A GREAT TRUMPET and THEY WILL GATHER TOGETHER His elect from the four winds, from one end of the sky to the other.**
> **32   "Now learn the parable from the fig tree: when its branch has already become tender, and puts forth its leaves, you know that summer is near;**
> **33   even so you too, when you see all these things, recognize that He is near, *right* at the door.**
> **34   "Truly I say to you, this generation will not pass away until all these things take place.**

35 "Heaven and earth will pass away, but My words shall not pass away.

36 "But of that day and hour no one knows, not even the angels of heaven, nor the Son, but the Father alone...."

—Matthew 24

Christ said that no one, not even Himself or angels, knows the day and the hour when the end of the age will occur. I say this very loudly and clearly: *WE CANNOT KNOW WHEN IT WILL OCCUR.* But, looking at the evidence and the way the Holy Spirit is warning those who believe in Jesus, I would have to conclude that there is a high probability that we are living in the last days of this present age, and we could well see the return of Christ.

We cannot know for certain when the Lord's return will be, but, as Christians, we have a responsibility to have a general idea of when it might be. I think that this is pointed out very beautifully in this passage:

1 Now as to the times and the epochs, brethren, you have no need of anything to be written to you.

2 For you yourselves know full well that the day of the Lord will come just like a thief in the night.

3 While they are saying, "Peace and safety!" then destruction will come upon them suddenly like birth pangs upon a woman with child; and they shall not escape.

4 But you, brethren, are not in darkness, that the day should overtake you like a thief;

5 for you are all sons of light and sons of day. We are not of night nor of darkness;

6 so then let us not sleep as others do, but let us be alert and sober.

—1 Thessalonians 5

I particularly would like to call your attention to verse 4 of the passage above. It states that, as brothers in Christ, we are not in the darkness, and the day should not overtake us like a thief—as it will the rest of the world. I do not believe this means that we will know exactly when Christ will return, but that—by the prophecies in the Scriptures and the witness of the Holy Spirit to our hearts—we should have a good idea of the times and the seasons in which we live. Verse 6 admonishes us to be in a state of readiness for the Lord's return.

Let me restate what we have just covered. For non-Christians, the Lord's coming will be like the coming of a thief in the night; it will catch them totally unaware. But, as Christians, we should not be overtaken as by a thief. We should not be surprised by the return of Christ!

We have just seen that we cannot know when the end of this age will occur. We saw earlier in this book that the rapture will occur on the last day of this age (Chapter 5). The passage we read near the beginning of this chapter foretold of what it would be like in the "last days" and that these days would culminate with the return of the Son of God. In spite of the uncertainty concerning the timing, we are commanded in the Scriptures to be ready:

> **40   "You too, be ready; for the Son of Man is coming at an hour that you do not expect.**
>
> **—Luke 12**

In Matthew 24 we have the answer that Christ gave in response to the disciples' question of what the signs of the end of the age and of His coming would be. If we read that chapter in its entirety, we find that it does not in any place refer to a pre-tribulation rapture. Towards the end of that chapter, Christ said to His disciples:

> **42   "Therefore be on the alert, for you do not know which day your Lord is coming...."**
>
> **—Matthew 24**

We are to be on the alert *BECAUSE* we do not know when the Lord is coming back. He obviously was not talking about being prepared for a pre-tribulation rapture, since He had not discussed one. He must be telling us to be alert and ready for His return at the end of the tribulation.

I think that one of the best summaries of what we are talking about is found in Mark:

32 "But of that day or hour no one knows, not even the angels in heaven, nor the Son, but the Father *alone.*

33 "Take heed, keep on the alert; for you do not know when the *appointed* time is.

34 "It is like a man, away on a journey, who upon leaving his house and putting his slaves in charge, *assigning* to each one his task, also commanded the doorkeeper to stay on the alert.

35 "Therefore, be on the alert—for you do not know when the master of the house is coming, whether in the evening, at midnight, at cockcrowing, or in the morning—

36 lest he come suddenly and find you asleep.

37 "And what I say to you I say to all, 'Be on the alert!'"

—Mark 13

SUMMARY AND CONCLUSION

We have further seen that we cannot know when Christ will return, but we are commanded in the Scriptures to be on the alert and to be ready for it. Since the tribulation will likely begin in a gradual way, rather than on a specific day, we cannot say, for example, that the Lord's coming is seven years after some particular event. Thus, Christ's words that He will come like a thief in the night are certainly true. His return—to end the tribulation—is what has been referred to throughout the centuries as the "blessed hope" of Christians. We talk a great deal about faith and love, but most of us forget the third member of that trinity—*HOPE*. Perhaps this is because we have life so easy. However, in the rougher times that are ahead, hope will become a very important aspect to Christians.

We then saw that, although we cannot know when His return will be, the Holy Spirit appears to be moving worldwide, showing believers that we are in the end times (last days of this present age) and warning us to prepare. If this is indeed a work of the Holy Spirit, He could be saying to Christians (the body of Christ) that we are to get ready spiritually and physically for the tribulation, which we will experience.

END-TIMES NEWS DIGEST

It is impossible in a book always to be totally up-to-date on everything concerning the end times of this age. To help keep you current on the end times and current events that relate to prophecy, Omega Ministries publishes a newsletter called *End-Times News Digest*. It has blessed hundreds of thousands of people around the world and is acclaimed by prophecy teachers of all persuasions.

If you would like to receive a free six-month subscription to *End-Times News Digest*, you can write to:

Omega Ministries
P.O. Box 1788
Medford, OR 97501

Another option is to tear out the last page of this book and send it in to them.

12

POWER AND PEACE
IN THE END TIMES

Even though we have seen that we are very likely the generation that will go through the end of this age and experience the great tribulation, in no way should we face this with a sense of gloom and doom or anxiety. If we are bondslaves of God, through Jesus Christ, then we will go through it with real power and peace. We will have God's divine protection and we will experience major victories through the end of this age.

I would like to emphasize that when I speak of bondslaves of God, I am *not* talking about elitism of any kind. I am *not* talking about some sort of an elite group of Christians who are above other Christians. *There is no such thing as a proud slave!*

The term "bondslave" refers to people who have humbled themselves, who are willing to be slaves to God the Father, and to serve Him and the body of Christ. I am talking about a servant company, not an elite company.

God is going to do a new thing on the earth. He is doing a fresh dividing. There began to be a dividing in large proportions, starting in the 1960's. There were some Christians who were willing to humble themselves and be baptized with the Holy Spirit. These were willing to be made fools of for God's sake and even to do "foolish" things, in the eyes of the world. However, to those who were willing to submit to God in this way, God gave many gifts, such as the gift of healing. These supernatural gifts had not been experienced widely by Christians in recent centuries.

Now God is doing a new dividing: He is calling out from among this group those who are willing to humble themselves even further and become bondslaves of God the Father, through Jesus Christ. To this bondslave company He is going to give incredible power, not even experienced in the charismatic movement when it was at its height.

Before examining some of the power gifts that will be given to the bondslaves, let us take a look backward and see them in operation in the Old Testament.

FIRE FROM HEAVEN

I would like to share with you one of my favorite passages of Scripture which deals with Elijah calling down fire out of heaven. To help you get some of the background, we will need to read the introduction to the story:

> **2   And Ahaziah fell through the lattice in his upper chamber which *was* in Samaria, and became ill. So he sent messengers and said to them, "Go, inquire of Baalzebub, the god of Ekron, whether I shall recover from this sickness."**
>
> **3   But the angel of the Lord said to Elijah the Tishbite, "Arise, go up to meet the messengers of the king of Samaria and say to them, 'Is it because there is no God in Israel *that* you are going to inquire of Baalzebub, the god of Ekron?'**
>
> **4   "Now therefore thus says the Lord, 'You shall not come down from the bed where you have gone up, but you shall surely die.' " Then Elijah departed.**
>
> **5   When the messengers returned to him he said to them, "Why have you returned?"**
>
> **6   And they said to him, "A man came up to meet us and said to us, 'Go, return to the king who sent you and say to him, "Thus says the Lord, 'Is it because there is no God in Israel *that* you are sending to inquire of Baalzebub, the god of Ekron? Therefore you shall not come down from the bed where you have gone up, but shall surely die' " ' "**
>
> **7   And he said to them, "What kind of man was he who came up to meet you and spoke these words to you?"**

8   And they answered him, "He *was* a hairy man with a leather girdle bound about his loins." And he said, "It is Elijah the Tishbite."

—2 Kings 1

Here we see that the king had been injured and Elijah told the messengers to tell the king that he was going to die. This obviously did not make the king very happy. The king wanted Elijah brought to him. So here is what the king did:

9   Then *the king* sent to him a captain of fifty with his fifty. And he went up to him, and behold, he was sitting on the top of the hill. And he said to him, "O man of god, the king says, 'Come down.' "

10   And Elijah answered and said to the captain of fifty, "If I am a man of God, let fire come down from heaven and consume you and your fifty." Then fire came down from heaven and consumed him and his fifty.

11   So he again sent to him another captain of fifty with his fifty. And he answered and said to him, "O man of God, thus says the king, 'Come down quickly.' "

12   And Elijah answered and said to them, "If I am a man of God, let fire come down from heaven and consume you and your fifty." Then the fire of God came down from heaven and consumed him and his fifty.

13   So he again sent the captain of a third fifty with his fifty. When the third captain of fifty went up, he came and bowed down on his knees before Elijah, and begged him and said to him, "O man of God, please let my life and the lives of these fifty servants of yours be precious in your sight.

14   "Behold fire came down from heaven, and consumed the first two captains of fifty with their fifties; but now let my life be precious in your sight."

15   And the angel of the Lord said to Elijah, "Go down with him; do not be afraid of him." So he arose and went down with him to the king.

—2 Kings 1

Here we see that a captain and his platoon of soldiers came up to arrest Elijah, and Elijah called down fire from heaven which consumed them. Then a second captain and his platoon went up and, again, Elijah called down fire from heaven and killed them.

Lo and behold, a third captain with his fifty soldiers then came up. Now what would most Christians have done, had there previously been two identical situations and God had led them to call down fire from heaven both times? If a third, identical situation exhibited itself, most Christians would have called down fire from heaven and roasted that captain and his platoon before God could have stopped them. However, Elijah was a bondslave of God, allowing God to control his every action and his every word. Thus, when the third platoon came up, the angel said to go down with them, and so Elijah did. God can only give these power gifts to those He can absolutely trust.

We are all familiar with the contest between Elijah and the prophets of Baal to see if God was God or Baal was God. To refresh your memory, the story goes like this:

25   So Elijah said to the prophets of Baal, "Choose one ox for yourselves and prepare it first for you are many, and call on the name of your god, but put no fire *under* it."

26   Then they took the ox which was given them and they prepared it and called on the name of Baal from morning until noon saying, "O Baal, answer us." But there was no voice and no one answered. And they leaped about the alter which they made.

27   And it came about at noon, that Elijah mocked them and said, "Call out with a loud voice, for he is a god; either he is occupied or gone aside, or is on a journey, or perhaps he is asleep and needs to be awakened."

28   So they cried with a loud voice and cut themselves according to their custom with swords and lances until the blood gushed out on them.

29   And it came about when midday was past, that they raved until the time of the offering of the *evening* sacrifice; but there was no voice, no one answered, and no one paid attention.

30   Then Elijah said to all the people, "Come near to me." So all the people came near to him. And he repaired the altar of the Lord which had been torn down.

31   And Elijah took twelve stones according to the number of the tribes of the sons of Jacob, to whom the word of the Lord had come, saying, "Israel shall be your name."

32   So with the stones he built an altar in the name of the Lord, and he made a trench around the altar, large enough to hold two measures of seed.

33   Then he arranged the wood and cut the ox in pieces and laid *it* on the wood. And he said, "Fill four pitchers with water and pour *it* on the burnt offering and on the wood."

34   And he said, "Do it a second time," and they did it a second time. And he said, "Do it a third time," and they did it a third time.

35   And the water flowed around the altar, and he also filled the trench with water.

36   Then it came about at the time of the offering of the *evening* sacrifice, that Elijah the prophet came near and said, "O Lord, the God of Abraham, Isaac and Israel, today let it be known that Thou art God in Israel, and that I am Thy servant, and that I have done all these things at Thy word.

37   "Answer me, O Lord, answer me, that this people may know that Thou, O Lord, art God, and *that* Thou hast turned their heart back again."

38   Then the fire of the Lord fell, and consumed the burnt offering and the wood and the stones and the dust, and licked up the water that was in the trench.

39   And when the people saw it, they fell on their faces; and they said, "The Lord, He is God; the Lord, He is God."

40   Then Elijah said to them, "Seize the prophets of Baal; do not let one of them escape." So they seized them; and Elijah brought them down to the brook Kishon, and slew them there.

—1 Kings 18

Here again we see Elijah calling down fire from heaven. Instead of consuming soldiers, in this case, the fire consumed the sacrifice, the wood, the altar, and even the water in the trench!

I am not familiar with any Christian today to whom God has given this type of a power gift. However, as we will see a little later in this chapter, God is going to restore those power gifts to His bondslaves.

CONTROL OVER THE WEATHER

In the Old Testament, there is an instance recorded wherein Elijah caused there to be no rain upon the earth:

> **1   Now Elijah the Tishbite, who was of the settlers of Gilead, said to Ahab, "As the Lord, the God of Israel lives, before whom I stand, surely there shall be neither dew nor rain these years, except by my word."**
>
> **—1 Kings 17**

After the rain stopped, the Lord supernaturally provided for Elijah, the widow and her son, with whom Elijah made his abode during the time of famine resulting. Then, under God's command, Elijah restored rain to the earth:

> **1   Now it came about *after* many days, that the word of the Lord came to Elijah in the third year, saying, "Go, show yourself to Ahab, and I will send rain on the face of the earth."**
>
> **2   So Elijah went to show himself to Ahab. Now the famine *was* severe in Samaria....**
>
> **41   Now Elijah said to Ahab, "Go up, eat and drink; for there is a sound of the roar of a *heavy* shower."**
>
> **42   So Ahab went up to eat and drink. But Elijah went up to the top of Carmel; and he crouched down on the earth, and put his face between his knees.**
>
> **43   And he said to his servant, "Go up now, look toward the sea." So he went up and looked and said, "There is nothing." And he said, "Go back" seven times.**
>
> **44   And it came about at the seventh *time*, that he said, "Behold, a cloud as small as a man's hand is com-**

ing up from the sea." And he said, "Go up, say to Ahab,
'Prepare *your chariot* and go down, so that the *heavy*
shower does not stop you.' "

45   So it came about in a little while, that the sky
grew black with clouds and wind, and there was a heavy
shower. And Ahab rode and went to Jezreel.

46   Then the hand of the Lord was on Elijah, and he
girded up his loins and outran Ahab to Jezreel.

—1 Kings 18

Certainly, being able to control the weather is a power gift
that few Christians have ever even heard about. It is happening to a small degree at this point in time, but I believe it will
happen in a major way when God begins to restore the power
gifts to His bondslaves.

POWER TO BRING PLAGUES UPON THE EARTH

Moses—who was a bondslave of God—in obedience to
God, was able to bring plagues upon the earth:

1   Then the Lord said to Moses, "Go to Pharaoh and
say to him, 'Thus says the Lord, "Let My people go, that
they may serve Me.

2   "But if you refuse to let *them* go, behold, I will
smite your whole territory with frogs....

13   And the Lord did according to the word of Moses,
and the frogs died out of the houses, the courts, and the
fields.

—Exodus 8

8   Then the Lord said to Moses and Aaron, "Take for
yourselves handfuls of soot from a kiln, and let Moses
throw it toward the sky in the sight of Pharaoh.

9   "And it will become fine dust over all the land of
Egypt, and will become boils breaking out with sores
on man and beast through all the land of Egypt."

10   So they took soot from a kiln, and stood before
Pharaoh; and Moses threw it toward the sky, and it
became boils breaking out with sores on man and beast.

—Exodus 9

> 12   Then the Lord said to Moses, "Stretch out your hand over the land of Egypt for the locusts, that they may come up on the land of Egypt, and eat every plant of the land, *even* all that the hail has left."
>
> 13   So Moses stretched out his staff over the land of Egypt, and the Lord directed an east wind on the land all that day and all that night; and when it was morning, the east wind brought the locusts.
>
> 14   And the locusts came up over all the land of Egypt and settled in all the territory of Egypt; *they were* very numerous. There had never been so *many* locusts, nor would there be so *many* again....
>
> 21   Then the Lord said to Moses, "Stretch out your hand toward the sky, that there may be darkness over the land of Egypt, even a darkness which may be felt."
>
> 22   So Moses stretched out his hand toward the sky, and there was thick darkness in all the land of Egypt for three days.
>
> —Exodus 10

If God were to give someone who was not under His control, and who was not obedient to Him, power to bring plagues upon the earth, the earth could be a disastrous place in which to live. God can only entrust this type of spiritual power to those who are absolutely obedient to do what He says, when He says to do it—and nothing more and nothing less.

THOSE POWER GIFTS WILL BE RESTORED

It is exciting to know that those power gifts *are* going to be restored in a very dramatic way at the end of this age. We read about this in the book of Revelation:

> 3   "And I will grant *authority* to my two witnesses, and they will prophesy for twelve hundred and sixty days, clothed in sackcloth."
>
> 4   These are the two olive trees and the two lampstands that stand before the Lord of the earth.
>
> 5   And if anyone desires to harm them, fire proceeds out of their mouth and devours their enemies;

and if anyone would desire to harm them, in this manner he must be killed.

6   These have the power to shut up the sky, in order that rain may not fall during the days of their prophesying; and they have power over the waters to turn them into blood, and to smite the earth with every plague, as often as they desire.

—Revelation 11

These two witnesses may indeed be two individuals. On the other hand, they may be two companies of people. Whoever they are, I believe they are essentially going to be typical of God's bondslaves.

As we read in this passage, God will restore the power gifts to His witnesses—I believe, His bondslaves. If anyone intends to harm them physically, fire comes down and devours the enemy; it says, in this manner these enemies *must* be killed. Most Christians today would refuse to kill their enemies in this manner, because their knowledge of good and evil says that it is wrong to kill. If most Christians had been Elijah and God told them to call down fire from heaven to devour a captain and his platoon, they would have refused to have done so, because of their abhorrence for killing. Truthfully, I share this abhorrence for killing. I hope and pray that God will never ask me to kill another person. However, if I am going to be His bondslave, I must be willing to do anything that He tells me to do.

For example, consider Joshua at Jericho (Joshua 6:1-25). God commanded that, when the wall fell down, he and his men go forward and kill all the people—including pregnant women, little babies one day old, and old women. They were not to leave anyone alive, except Rahab and those in her house. Had we been there, most of us Christians would have argued with God that it was wrong to kill the little babies...perhaps we could raise them up and convert them. Most Christians today would have refused to have done what God commanded Joshua to do. I believe it was because Joshua was a bondslave, and most Christians today are not.

I use an extreme case as an example in order to make my point clear. As bondslaves of God, we must be willing to follow Him wherever He leads us, even if it is not comfortable, even it it is not "party line," even when it means laying down our own image of what is "right and wrong."

As we read in the passage from Revelation 11, God is also going to give His witnesses (His bondslaves) power to bring plagues upon the earth. These plagues are probably localized, as they were in Egypt with Moses, but God will command their use in order to achieve His purposes. His purposes may be to bring repentence or to bring judgment. However, His bondslaves may never know the reason why. They simply must act in obedience to God at the time God tells them to do something. But through their obedience, and through the power of God in bringing the plagues, the victory will be won for God, and God will get the glory. Isn't that exciting!

It also says that His witnesses (His bondslaves) will have the ability to cause it not to rain or to rain again. There have been some recent examples, two in my own life, wherein Christians have been utilized by God to actually control the weather.

There have been a number of recorded instances in which an evangelist was holding a major crusade in another country in an outdoor stadium. It would be raining on the day of the final meeting of the crusade and he would say publicly that: "The rain will stop by, say, 6:00." In every one of these instances, the rain has stopped, the meeting has taken place, and God got the glory.

There was a case of a young Chinese man who was traveling with a well-known Chinese teacher and evangelist. They went into this one area in which pagans were going to have a parade at noon honoring Buddha or the gods of some other religion. The young man pronounced to the public that it would rain at noon the next day.

Since this was not the rainy season and there was never rain this time of year, the people thought he was crazy. But sure enough, the next day it rained at noon and the parade could not be held. Then they announced that the parade would be held the following day. The young Chinese man again announced that on the next day it would rain again at 12:00, the time of the parade. Sure enough, it rained again the next day. They delayed the parade one more day, and the young man announced one final time that it would again rain on the following day at 12:00 noon. Of course, you know that God caused it to rain that next day, and He got the glory. These three days of consecutive rain occurred in the middle of the dry season. It made such an impact on that community that the halls were overflowing with people wanting to learn about this man's God and about Jesus Christ. The parade was never held. God triumphed in a dramatic display of His supernatural power through one obedient young Christian man.

Today, in the United States also, Christians—at the command of God—are taking dominion over nature. One example occurred in Illinois: a tornado was racing toward a small town. Most of the people in the town had rushed into storm cellars. A small group of Christians gathered on a front lawn and said to the tornado, "In the name of Jesus Christ, we command you not to strike our town."

What do you think happened? . . . The tornado lifted on the outskirts of the town, crossed high over, and hit the earth again, right past the town!

A similar thing happened to me. On June 30, 1976, my wife and I were having a wedding dedication service outside at her parents' home in Penticton, British Columbia. We were doing this purely for the glory of God, desiring to give a witness for Christ to her friends. Normally this was the dry season, but it had been raining almost steadily for two days. We had all been praying that the rain would stop, but still it continued.

The dedication was to start at 3:30 and about 2:00 I went outside in the rain, and walked around praying. As I was praying that the rain would stop, God said to me, "Prayer is not enough. I want you to take dominion over the rain." My reaction was, "Who—me?" It took me about fifteen minutes of confessing my sins and drawing close to God in the Holy Spirit, before I felt under His control and power enough to say, "Rain, in the name of Jesus Christ I command you to stop until after this wedding dedication is over." Praise God! Within an hour there was the most beautiful blue sky and sunshine, which remained all through the dedication and the dinner that followed, all of which was out-of-doors. Then, just as they were taking up the tablecloths, a few raindrops began to fall.

Now, I do not by any means suppose that I could go out just any old time and take dominion over the rain. It has to be when God tells us to do so, and we have to do it under *His* control. However, when He speaks to us, He expects us to obey and follow. The end result will always glorify Him!

We are beginning to see occasional glimpses of the power gifts returning. There is a new thing that the Holy Spirit is going to do. It will not be a renewed charismatic movement. It will be a completely new thing. In it, the power gifts of God are going to be poured out in abundance upon His bondslaves, as they are sealed on their foreheads with the seal of God, and thus protected from much of the plagues that are coming upon the earth, and protected from the mark of the beast.

WHAT IS THE SEAL OF GOD?

A number of years ago, I had the privilege of being the speaker at a large men's retreat in Manitoba, sponsored by the Alliance churches there. I ministered on the bondslaves of God and the seal of God. At the coffee break, a grey-headed Alliance pastor asked me if I had any idea what the seal of God was. I told him that the Scriptures did not clearly say, and I always like to differentiate "my opinion" from what the Scriptures clearly teach. So I said I would give him my opinion.

I reminded him that when Christ was on the Mount of Transfiguration, His face radiated the glory of God, as we read in Matthew:

1   And six days later Jesus took with Him Peter and James and John his brother, and brought them up to a high mountain themselves.
2   And He was transfigured before them; and His face shone like the sun, and His garments became as white as light.

—Matthew 17

Here we see that Jesus' face "shone like the sun." It radiated the Shekinah glory of God, because He had had such an
encounter with Father God. The same thing happened to
Moses in the Old Testament:

> **29   And it came about when Moses was coming down
> from Mount Sinai (and the two tablets of the testimony
> *were* in Moses' hand as he was coming down from the
> mountain), that Moses did not know that the skin of his
> face shone because of his speaking with Him.**
> **30   So when Aaron and all the sons of Israel saw
> Moses, behold, the skin of his face shone, and they were
> afraid to come near him.**
>
> **—Exodus 34**

In talking about those who have "insight," Daniel had this
to say:

> **3   And those who have insight will shine brightly
> like the brightness of the expanse of heaven, and those
> who lead the many to righteousness, like the stars for-
> ever and ever.**
>
> **—Daniel 12**

Jesus said that the righteous were going to shine forth as
the sun:

> **41   "The Son of Man will send forth His angels, and
> they will gather out of His Kingdom all stumbling
> blocks, and those who commit lawlessness,**
> **42   and will cast them into the furnace of fire; in that
> place there shall be weeping and gnashing of teeth.**
> **43   "Then THE RIGHTEOUS WILL SHINE FORTH AS
> THE SUN in the kingdom of their Father. He who has
> ears, let him hear...."**
>
> **—Matthew 13**

I shared with this wise Alliance minister that it is possible that the bondslaves of God are going to have such an
encounter with Father God that their faces will radiate the
Shekinah glory of God. I seriously doubt that the seal of God
will be a tattoo or a rubber stamp on our foreheads that we
can comb our hair down over and hide. Very likely, we will

be the "sons of light," with our faces radiating His glory, and therefore all will know that it is *God* doing the miraculous deeds through us at the end of the age. No glory will go to any bondslave or overcomer; all the glory will go to Jesus and God the Father.

I do not know if the seal of God will be this or something even more wonderful. Whatever it is, I am willing to make any sacrifice now in order to have it during the end times of this age.

"THREE SPIRITUAL R'S"

We have covered a lot of ground in this book, perhaps touching on some subjects that are new to you. We all see through a glass darkly (1 Corinthians 13:12), and I certainly would not claim to have all of the answers, particularly when it comes to prophecy. What I have tried to do in this book is to share with you what God has shown me up to this point in my life and walk with Him. I pray that He will continue to enlighten me and clarify more and more of the Scriptures to me every day. I pray that He does the same for you as well.

I do believe that there have been some teachings made popular in recent years that have done damage to the body of Christ. In this book, I have tried to clear up some of those misinterpretations that can prevent us from being all that God wants us, His people, to be.

I would encourage you to be like the Berean Christians in their response to the ministry of Paul and Silas. The Scriptures tell us this:

> **11   Now these were more noble-minded than those in Thessalonica, for they received the word with great eagerness, examining the Scriptures daily, to *see* whether these things were so.**
>
> **12   Many of them therefore believed, along with a number of prominent Greek women and men.**
>
> **—Acts 17**

We learn here that the Bereans did three things:

1.   They received the word with great eagerness
2.   They examined the Scriptures daily, to see whether these things were so
3.   Many therefore believed (responded with their lives)

A simple way to remember this is as what I like to call the "three spiritual R's":

1.   Receptivity
2.   Research
3.   Response

If any one of those elements is missing, you can get into trouble. If you are not receptive, how can God possibly teach you new things? If you do not then take what you have been taught and do your own research, you can easily be led astray by false teachings that inevitably will come. And if, when God has made something real to you, you do not, in turn, respond with your life, what good is it to you?

It is my prayer that this will be your response to this book. I pray that:

1.   You will first be receptive to the possibly new ideas presented herein.
2.   You will be diligent to check out even what I say to see if it matches with the Scriptures.
3.   You will allow the Holy Spirit to quicken to you that which is truth and to make real what changes He would have you to make in your life. Then be obedient to make those changes.

Perhaps the Lord will speak to you about making a commitment to Him to become a bondslave of His. There is no greater adventure than giving all of your life to the Lord and seeing what He does with you, in you and through you! For your convenience, the next to the last page of this book is a bondslave commitment to help you pray through that commitment to God.

JUST AS IN THE DAYS OF GIDEON

God used Gideon to deliver Israel from the enemy. This is a record of his exciting adventure:

2 And the Lord said to Gideon, "The people who are with you are too many for Me to give Midian into their hands, lest Israel become boastful, saying, 'My own power has delivered me.'

3 "Now therefore come, proclaim in the hearing of the people, saying, 'Whoever is afraid and trembling, let him return and depart from Mount Gilead.' " So 22,000 people returned, but 10,000 remained.

4 Then the Lord said to Gideon, "The people are still too many; bring them down to the water and I will test them for you there. Therefore it shall be that he of whom I say to you, 'This one shall go with you,' he shall go with you; but everyone of whom I say to you, 'This one shall not go with you,' he shall not go."

5 So he brought the people down to the water. And the Lord said to Gideon, "You shall separate everyone who laps the water with his tongue, as a dog laps, as well as everyone who kneels to drink."

6 Now the number of those who lapped, putting their hand to their mouth, was 300 men; but all the rest of the people kneeled to drink water.

7 And the Lord said to Gideon, "I will deliver you with the 300 men who lapped and will give the Midianites into your hands; so let all the *other* people go, each man to his home."

8 So the 300 men took the people's provisions and their trumpets into their hands. And Gideon sent all the *other* men of Israel, each to his tent, but retained the 300 men; and the camp of Midian was below him in the valley....

16 And he divided the 300 men into three companies, and he put trumpets and empty pitchers into the hands of all of them, with torches inside the pitchers.

17 And he said to them, "Look at me, and do likewise. And behold, when I come to the outskirts of the camp, do as I do.

18 "When I and all who are with me blow the trumpet, then you also blow the trumpets all around the camp, and say, 'For the Lord and for Gideon.' "

19 So Gideon and the hundred men who were with him came to the outskirts of the camp at the beginning of the middle watch, when they had just posted the watch; and they blew the trumpets and smashed the pitchers that were in their hands.

20 When the three companies blew the trumpets and broke the pitchers, they held the torches in their left hands and the trumpets in their right hands for blowing, and cried, "A sword for the Lord and for Gideon!"

21 And each stood in his place around the camp, and all the army ran, crying out as they fled.

—Judges 7

As we read this, we see that initially there were 32,000 in Gideon's army. God said that was too many, lest Israel become self-reliant. So when Gideon told everyone to go home who did not want to be there, only 10,000 were left. Out of those 10,000, only 300 could be trusted to be absolutely obedient (bondslaves).

A similar separating could easily occur today. Think of this situation. Suppose there were three auditoriums of equal size. One of them had a Christian singing group. Another auditorium had a "miracle and healing service" and the third auditorium had someone teaching on how to live holy, pure and righteous before God. What do you think would happen if 32,000 Christians were turned loose and told that they could go to any of the three auditoriums? Probably 22,000 would go to hear the singing group; maybe some 10,000 would go to the miracle and healing service, and very likely only about 300 would go to hear the teaching on how to live pure, holy and righteous before God. Things have not changed at all. They are the same today as they were in the day of Gideon.

Drawing a parallel to our situation today, out of 32,000 born-again Christians, probably about 10,000 are filled with the Holy Spirit. However, many of that 10,000 who are filled with the Holy Spirit are living carnal lives. Most of them are likely living somewhat self-centered lives, and probably only about 300 are willing to be true bondslaves of God.

You might wish to pray about which category you fall into. The bondslaves are the people that God is going to empower to go through the end of this age victoriously as overcomers. If you want to have victory during the end of this age, I would strongly encourage you to become a bondslave of God, through Jesus Christ our Lord and Savior.

ADDITIONAL POWER IN A GROUP

Through the centuries, God has used His church—a group of believers, not a building—to achieve His purposes. As the end times of this age progress, God is going to use His church more than ever. The gifts of the Holy Spirit are given for the purpose of building up the church. Thus, the Holy Spirit has no reason to give these gifts to anyone who is not part of a local body of believers, a local church.

We also know from the Bible that where a group of people are praying together, there is additional spiritual power:

19 "Again I say to you, that if two of you agree on earth about anything that they may ask, it shall be done for them by My Father who is in heaven.
20 "For where two or three have gathered together in My name, there I am in their midst."
—Matthew 18

Here Jesus promised that where even two or three are gathered together in His name, He would be there. We do not even have to ask Him for His presence. He said He would be there whether we ask Him or not. Praise the Lord! It is exciting that Jesus Himself is at every gathering of believers.

As the church prayed fervently for Peter when he was in prison, the Lord answered and sent an angel to deliver him:

5 So Peter was kept in the prison, but prayer for him was being made fervently by the church of God.

6   And on the very night when Herod was about to bring him forward, Peter was sleeping between two soldiers, bound with two chains; and guards in front of the door were watching over the prison.

7   And behold, an angel of the Lord suddenly appeared, and a light shone in the cell; and he struck Peter's side and roused him, saying, "Get up quickly." And his chains fell off his hands.

8   And the angel said to him, "Gird yourself and put on your sandals." And he did so. And he said to him, "Wrap your cloak around you and follow me."

9   And he went out and continued to follow, and he did not know that what was being done by the angel was real, but thought he was seeing a vision.

10   And when they had passed the first and second guard, they came to the iron gate that leads into the city, which opened for them by itself; and they went out and went along one street; and immediately the angel departed from him.

11   And when Peter came to himself, he said, "Now I know for sure that the Lord has sent forth His angel and rescued me from the hand of Herod and from all that the Jewish people were expecting."

—Acts 12

As we meet together and pray, there is an additional power in our prayers, above and beyond that which we have as individuals. When we meet together and praise and worship as a group of believers, the Bible tells us that God inhabits the praises of His people (Psalm 22:3); out of His very presence come forth healings, miracles and anointed words and teachings. Jesus did not establish a bunch of "lone ranger" individuals. He established His church, a body of believers.

Much of what we have talked about in this book has dealt with the individual, but, in many cases, it can also be applied to a group of believers. We are going to need each other in the end times. We are going to need to be committed to Christ as the total Master of our lives. We will also need to be committed to each other, to help and support one another during times of crisis. If we do this, we will indeed have victory—victory through Jesus.

VICTORY IN CHRIST

During the end of this age, there is no way that you and I will be strong enough to stand against the attacks of Satan by ourselves. However, we can and will have victory through Jesus Christ. In the first place, we need to remind ourselves that Christ is greater than Satan:

> **1   Beloved, do not believe every spirit, but test the spirits to see whether they are from God; because many false prophets have gone out into the world.**
> **2   By this you know the Spirit of God: every spirit that confesses that Jesus Christ has come in the flesh is from God;**
> **3   and every spirit that does not confess Jesus is not from God; and this is the spirit of the antichrist, of which you have heard that it is coming, and now it is already in the world.**
> **4   You are from God, little children, and have overcome them; because greater is He who is in you than he who is in the world.**
>
> **—1 John 4**

All the works of Satan are going to be totally destroyed and demolished. Praise the glorious and powerful name of Jesus!

> **7   Little children, let no one deceive you; the one who practices righteousness is righteous, just as He is righteous;**
> **8   the one who practices sin is of the devil; for the devil has sinned from the beginning. The Son of God appeared for this purpose, that He might destroy the works of the devil.**
>
> **—1 John 3**

Christ is not only going to destroy the works of Satan, but He is going to destory all rule and all authority and all power.

There will be no governments left, no policemen, no military. Christ alone will have power:

24   then *comes* the end, when He delivers up the kingdom to the God and Father, when He has abolished all rule and all authority and power.

—1 Corinthians 15

Christ is a Lord of triumph and victory. He shows His power and His victory through us as we conquer in His name.

14   But thanks be to God, who always leads us in His triumph in Christ, and manifests through us the sweet aroma of the knowledge of Him in every place.

—2 Corinthians 2

We are not just barely victors and conquerors in Jesus Christ. The following verse tells us that we are far "more than conquerors" (*KJV*). We *overwhelmingly* conquer!

35   Who shall separate us from the love of Christ? Shall tribulation, or distress, or persecution, or famine, or nakedness, or peril, or sword?
36   Just as it is written,
"FOR THY SAKE WE ARE BEING PUT TO DEATH ALL DAY LONG;
WE WERE CONSIDERED AS SHEEP TO BE SLAUGHTERED."
37   But in all these things we overwhelmingly conquer through Him who loved us.

—Romans 8

As we conclude this work, I pray for you what Paul prayed for the Christians at Ephesus:

18   I pray that the eyes of your heart may be enlightened, so that you may know what is the hope of His calling, what are the riches of the glory of His inheritance in the saints,
19   and what is the surpassing greatness of His power toward us who believe. These are in accordance with the working of the strength of His might

20   which He brought about in Christ, when He raised Him from the dead, and seated Him at His right hand in the heavenly places,

21   far above all rule and authority and power and dominion, and every name that is named, not only in this age, but also in the one to come.

—Ephesians 1

A

HOW TO BECOME A CHRISTIAN

If you are reading this, I am assuming that you are not sure that you have received Jesus Christ as your personal Savior. Not only is it possible to know this for sure, but God wants you to know. The following is what 1 John 5 has to say:

11   And the witness is this, that God has given us eternal life, and this life is in His Son.
12   He who has the Son has the life; he who does not have the Son does not have the life.
13   These things I have written to you who believe in the name of the Son of God, in order that you may know that you have eternal life.

These things are written to us who believe in the name of the Son of God, so that we can know that we have eternal life. It is not a "guess so," or "hope so" or "maybe so" situation. It is so that we can know for certain that we have eternal life. If you do not have this confidence, please read on.

In order to get to the point of knowing that we have eternal life, we need to go back and review some basic principles. First, it is important to note that all things that God created (the stars, trees, animals, and so on) are doing exactly what they were created to do, except man. Isaiah 43 indicates why God created us:

7   "...Everyone who is called by My name,
And whom I have created for My glory,
Whom I have formed even whom I have made."

Here it says that humans were created to glorify God. I am sure that neither you nor I have glorified God all of our lives in everything that we have done. This gives us our first clue as to what "sin" is. We find more about it in Romans 3:

23   for all have sinned and fall short of the glory of God,...

This says that we have all sinned and that we all fall short of the purpose for which we were created—that of glorifying God. I have an even simpler definition of sin. I believe that sin is "living independent of God." A young person out of high school can choose which college to attend. If he makes this decision apart from God, it is "sin." This was the basic problem in the garden of Eden. Satan tempted Eve to eat the fruit of the tree of "the knowledge of good and evil." He said that if she would do this, she would know good from evil and would be wise like God. This would mean that she could make her own decisions and would not have to rely on God's wisdom and guidance. Since you and I fit in the category of living independent of God and not glorifying Him in everything we do, we need to look at what the results of this sin are.

First let me ask you what "wages" are. After thinking about it, because you probably receive wages from your job, you will probably come up with a definition something like "wages are what you get paid for what you do." That is a good answer. Now let's see what the Bible has to say concerning this:

23   For the wages of sin is death, but the free gift of God is eternal life in Christ Jesus our Lord.
—Romans 6

Here we see that the wages of sin is death—spiritual, eternal death. Death is what we get paid for the sin that we do. Yet this passage also gives us the other side of the coin: that is, that through Jesus Christ we can freely have eternal life, instead of eternal death. Isn't that wonderful?!

But let's return for a moment to this death penalty that the people without Christ have hanging over their heads, because of the sin that they live in. In the Old Testament God made a rule: "The soul who sins will die" (Ezekiel 18:4). If we were able to live a perfect, sinless life, we could make it to heaven on our own. If we live anything less than a perfect life, according to God's rule, we will not make it to heaven, but instead will be sentenced to death. All through the Bible we find no one living a good enough life to make it to heaven.

This brings us to the place where Jesus Christ fits into this whole picture. His place was beautifully illustrated to me when I was considering receiving Christ as my Savior, by a story about a judge in a small town.

In this small town, the newspapermen were against the judge and wanted to get him out of office. A case was coming up before the judge concerning a vagrant—a drunken bum—who happened to have been a fraternity brother of the judge when they were at college. The newspapermen thought that this was their chance. If the judge let the vagrant off easy, the headlines would read, "Judge Shows Favoritism to Old Fraternity Brother." If the judge gave the vagrant the maximum penalty, the headlines would read, "Hardhearted Judge Shows No Mercy to Old Fraternity Brother." Either way they had him. The judge heard the case and gave the vagrant the maximum penalty of thirty days or $300 fine.

The judge then stood up, took off his robe, laid it down on his chair, walked down in front of the bench and put his arm around the shoulders of his old fraternity brother. He told him that as judge, in order to uphold the law, he had to give him the maximum penalty, because he was guilty. But because he cared about him, he wanted to pay the fine for him. So the judge took out his wallet and handed his old fraternity brother $300.

For God to be "just," He has to uphold the law that says "the soul who sins will die." On the other hand, because He loves us He wants to pay that death penalty for us. I cannot pay the death penalty for you because I have a death penalty of my own that I have to worry about, since I, too, have sinned. If I were sinless, I could die in your place. I guess God could have sent down millions of sinless beings to die for us. But what God chose to do was to send down one Person, who was equal in value, in God's eyes, to all of the people who will ever live, and yet who would remain sinless. Jesus Christ died physically and spiritually in order to pay the death penalty for you and me. The blood of Christ washes away all of our sins, and with it the death penalty that resulted from our sin.

The judge's old fraternity brother could have taken the $300 and said thank you, or he could have told the judge to keep his money and that he would do it on his own. Similarly, each person can thank God for allowing Christ to die in his place and receive Christ as his own Savior, or he can tell God to keep His payment and that he will make it on his own. What you do with that question determines where you will spend eternity.

Referring to Christ, John 1 says this:

12   But as many as received Him, to them He gave the right to become children of God, even to those who believe in His name...

John 3:16 says:

16   "For God so loved the world, that He gave His only begotten son, that whoever believes in Him should not perish but have eternal life...."

Here we see that if we believe in Christ we won't perish, but we will have everlasting life and the right to become children of God. Right now you can tell God that you believe in Christ as the Son of God, that you are sorry for your sins and that you want to turn from them. You can tell Him that you want to accept Christ's payment for your sins, and yield your life to be controlled by Christ and the Holy Spirit. (You must accept Christ as your Savior *and your MASTER*.)

If you pray such a prayer, Christ will come and dwell within your heart and you will know for sure that you have eternal life.

If you have any questions about what you have just read, I would encourage you to go to someone that you know, who really knows Jesus Christ as his Savior, and ask him for help and guidance. After you receive Christ, I would encourage you to become a part of a group of believers in Christ who study the Scriptures together, worship God together and have a real love relationship with each other. This group (body of believers) can help nurture you and build you up in your new faith in Jesus Christ.

If you have received Christ as a result of reading these pages, I would love to hear from you. My address is at the end of this book.

Welcome to the family of God.

James McKeever

B

MARGARET MACDONALD'S ACCOUNT

The information in this Appendix is quoted from Dave McPherson's book, *The Incredible Cover-Up.*

[This is Margaret Macdonald's handwritten account of her 1830 Pre-Trib revelation, as included in Robert Norton's *Memoirs of James & George Macdonald, of Port-Glasgow* (1840), pp. 171-176. The italicized portions represent her account as it appears in shorter form in Norton's *The Restoration of Apostles and Prophets; In the Catholic Apostolic Church* (1861), pp. 15-18.]

"It was first the awful state of the land that was pressed upon me. I saw the blindness and infatuation of the people to be very great. I felt the cry of Liberty just to be the hiss of the serpent, to drown them in perdition. It was just 'no God.' I repeated the words, Now there is distress of nations, with perplexity, the seas and the waves roaring, men's hearts failing them for fear—now look out for the sign of the Son of man. Here I was made to stop and cry out, O it is not known what the sign of the Son of man is; the people of God think they are waiting, but they know not what it is. *I felt this needed to be revealed, and that there was great darkness and error about it; but suddenly what it was burst upon me with a glorious light. I saw it was just the Lord himself descending from Heaven with a shout, just the glorified man, even Jesus; but that all must, as Stephen was, be filled with the Holy Ghost, that they might look up, and see the brightness of the Father's glory. I saw the error to be, that men think that it will be something seen by the natural eye; but 'tis spiritual discernment that is needed, the eye of God in his people. Many passages were revealed, in a light in which I had not before seen them. I repeated, 'Now is the kingdom of Heaven like unto ten virgins, who went forth to meet the Bridegroom, five wise and five foolish*; they that were foolish took their lamps, but took no oil with them; but they that were wise took oil in their vessels with the lamps.' 'But *be ye not unwise, but understanding what the will of the Lord is; and be not drunk with wine* wherein is excess, *but be filled with the Spirit.*' This was the oil the wise virgins took in their *vessels—this is the light to be kept burning—the light of God— that we may discern that which cometh not with observation to the natural eye. Only those who have the light of God within them will see the sign of his appearance. No need to follow them who say, see here, or see there, for his day shall be as the light-ning to those in whom the living Christ is.* 'Tis Christ in us that will lift us up—he is the light—'tis only those that are alive in him that will be caught up to meet him in the air. *I saw that we must be in the Spirit, that we might see spiritual things. John was in the spirit, when he saw a throne set in Heaven.—But I saw that the glory of the ministration of the Spirit had not been known. I repeated frequently, but the spiritual temple must and shall be reared, and the fulness of Christ be poured into his body, and then shall we be caught up to meet him.* Oh *none will be counted worthy of this calling but his body,* which is *the church,* and which must be *a candlestick all of gold.* I often said, *Oh the glorious inbreaking of God* which is *Now about to burst on this earth;* Oh *the glorious temple* which is *now about to be reared, the bride adorned for her husband; and Oh what a holy, holy bride she must be, to be prepared for such a glorious bridegroom.* I said, Now shall the people of God have to do with realities—*now shall the glorious mystery of God in our nature be known—now shall it be known what it is for man to be glorified.* If felt that the revelation of Jesus Christ had yet to be opened up—it is not knowledge about God that it con-tains, but it is an entering into God—I saw that there was a glori-ous breaking in of God to be. *I felt as Elijah, surrounded with chariots of fire. I saw as it were, the spiritual temple reared, and the Head Stone brought forth with shoutings of grace, grace, unto it. It was a glorious light above the brightness of the sun, that shone round about me. I felt that those who were filled with the Spirit could see spiritual things, and feel walk-ing in the midst of them, while those who had not the Spirit could see nothing—so that two shall be in one bed, the one taken and the other left,* because the one has the light of God within while the other cannot see the Kingdom of Heaven. *I saw the people of God in an awfully dangerous situation,* surrounded by nets and entanglements, about to be tried, and many about to be deceived and fall. *Now will THE WICKED be revealed, with all power and signs and lying wonders, so that if it were possible the very elect will be deceived.*—This is the fiery trial which is to try us.—It will be for the purging and purifying of the real members of the body of Jesus; but Oh *it will be a fiery trial. Every soul will be shaken to the very centre.* The enemy will try to shake in every thing we have believed— *but the trial of real faith will be found to honour and praise and glory. Nothing but what is of God will stand. The stony-ground hearers will be made manifest—the love of many will wax cold.* I frequently *said* that night, and often since, *now shall the awful sight of a false Christ be seen on this earth, and nothing but* the living *Christ in us can detect this awful attempt of the enemy to deceive—for it is with all deceivableness of unrighteousness he will work—he will have a counterpart for every part of God's truth, and an imitation for every work of the Spirit.* The Spirit must and will be poured out on the church, that she may be purified and filled with God—and just *in proportion as the Spirit of God works, so will be—when our Lord anoints men with power, so will he. This is* particularly the nature of *the trial, through which those are to pass who will be counted worthy to stand before the Son of man. There will be outward trial too, but 'tis principally temptation. It is brought on by the outpouring of the Spirit, and will just increase in proportion as the Spirit is poured out.* The trial of the Church is from Antichrist. It is by being filled with the Spirit that we shall be kept. *I frequently said, Oh be filled with the Spirit—have the light of God in you, that you may detect satan—be full of eyes within—be clay in the hands of the potter—submit to be filled,* filled *with God.* This will build the temple. *It is not by might nor by power, but by my Spirit, saith the Lord. This will fit us to enter into the marriage supper of the Lamb. I saw it to be the will of God that all should be filled. But what hindered the* real *life of God from being received by his people, was their turning from Jesus,* who is the way to the Father. They were not entering in by the door. For he is faithful who hath said, by me if any man enter in he shall find pasture.

They were *passing the cross, through which every drop of the Spirit of God flows to us.* All power that comes not through the blood of Christ is not of God. When I say, they are looking from the cross, I feel that there is much in it—they turn from the blood of the Lamb, by which we overcome, and in which our robes are washed and made white. There are low views of God's holiness, and a ceasing to condemn sin in the flesh, and a looking from him who humbled himself, and made himself of no reputation. *Oh! it is* needed, *much needed* at present, *a leading back to the cross. I saw that night, and often since, that there will be an outpouring of the Spirit* on the body, *such as has not been, a baptism of fire, that all the dross may be put away.* Oh there must and will be such an indwelling of the living God as has not been—*the servants of God sealed in their foreheads*—great conformity to Jesus—*his holy* holy *image* seen *in his people*—just *the bride made comely, by his comeliness put upon her.* This is what we are at present made to pray much for, that speedily we may all be made ready to meet our Lord in the air—and it will be. *Jesus wants his bride. His desire is toward us. He that shall come, will come, and will not tarry.* Amen and Amen. Even so come Lord Jesus."

—pp. 151-154

The remainder of this Appendix is Dave MacPherson's comments on Margaret Macdonald's vision and the ramifications of it.

Several observations are in order:

First of all, she evidently did not believe in imminence; she thought that "the fulness of Christ" (Spirit-filling) was first necessary—"and then shall we be caught up to meet him." She said that the catching up (or Rapture) would be seen only by Spirit-filled believers—a secret coming.

She equated the "sign of the Son of man" (which is in a Post-Trib setting in Matt. 24:30) with "the Lord himself descending from Heaven with a shout" (1 Thess. 4:16). Either her Tribulation occurs in a short space at the very end of the age (highly unlikely considering the fiery trial that would purge those in the church "who had not the Spirit"), or else she thought that the sign of the Son of man, though unseen by the world, will be seen by Spirit-filled believers before "THE WICKED be revealed"; she apparently believed the latter interpretation.

When she spoke of "one taken and the other left" it was not a separation of believers and unbelievers but rather Spirit-filled believers taken while believers not filled with the Spirit are left. But the point is this: some are to be taken (in a Rapture) *before* "THE WICKED" (or Antichrist) is revealed; when she used the term "Now" in her expression "Now will THE WICKED be revealed," she meant "later" or "after this" and was using this term sequentially. (J.N. Darby used the same word in the same way in his quote in the fifth chapter of this book: "Now He was Himself manifested....")

Margaret believed that a select group of believers would be raptured from the earth before the days of Antichrist, but also saw other believers enduring the Tribulation; she divided up the last generation of believers while Darby at least kept the church intact—but exempted all of the church from the Tribulation. In footnote 5 in chapter 5, Robert Norton elaborated on the doctrine that sprang from Margaret's revelation, and in chapter 6 he declared that Margaret's statement was the first instance of two-stage teaching.

The above evidence in published form has been shared in recent months with evangelical scholars around the world. In his book *The Church and the Tribulation,* Westmont College professor Robert H. Gundry originally leaned toward Edward Irving as the pre-trib originator. (His latest printing, however, deleted all of his Irving support and substituted the facts about Margaret Macdonald as found in this book.)

Later on J. Barton Payne described our evidence, in an *Evangelical Theological Society Journal* review, as "the most in-depth study yet to be made available on the historical origins of pretribulationism." *The Witness,* oldest and largest Darbyist Brethren magazine in England, admitted in a review last year that the above evidence "succeeds in establishing that the view outlined was first stated by a certain Margaret Macdonald"—despite those who still say that the Apostle Paul was first. And F.F. Bruce recently summed up our discoveries in *the Evangelical Quarterly* as a "valuable and racy narrative, which students of nineteenth-century prophetic interpretation are bound to take seriously."

Since Margaret Macdonald was the first person to teach a coming of Christ that would precede the days of Antichrist, it necessarily follows that Darby—back to whom pre-tribism can easily be traced—was at least second or third or even farther on down the line. To date no solid evidence has been found that proves that anyone other than this young Scottish lassie was the first person to teach a future coming of Christ before the days of Antichrist. Before 1830 Christians had always believed in a single future coming, that the catching up of 1 Thess. 4 will take place after the Great Tribulation of Matthew 24 at the glorious coming of the Son of man when He shall send His angels to gather together all of His elect.

Whether she realized it or not, Margaret did her part to pave the way for doctrine that would demand separate waiting rooms at the end of this age—one for the church and another one for Israel!

Finally, to charge that Darby could never have been influenced by Margaret's pre-Antichrist rapture, with the knowledge of her revelation and his whereabouts in 1830 now out in the open, is practically the same as saying that a man found with a smoking revolver in hand and standing over a freshly killed victim in the middle of a lonely desert could not possibly be a suspect!

—pp. 154-156

C

MEET THE AUTHOR

Dr. James McKeever is an international consulting economist, lecturer, author, world traveler, and Bible teacher. His financial consultations are utilized by scores of individuals from all over the world who seek his advice on investment strategy and international affairs.

Dr. McKeever is the editor and major contributing writer of the *McKeever Strategy Letter,* an economic and investment letter with worldwide circulation and recognition, rated #1 for 1985 and 1986 by an independent newsletter-rating service, and showing an average profit of 71 percent per year over the last nine years (1978-1986). He is also editor of the *Mutual Fund Advantage* newsletter, which helps the smaller investor profit from the increasingly-popular area of mutual funds.

Dr. McKeever has been a featured speaker at monetary, gold and tax haven conferences in London, Zurich, Bermuda, Amsterdam, South Africa, Australia, Singapore and Hong Kong, as well as all over the North American continent and Latin America.

As an economist and futurist, Dr. McKeever has shared the platform with such men as Ronald Reagan, Gerald Ford, William Simon, William Buckley, Alan Greenspan, heads of foreign governments, and many other outstanding thinkers.

For five years after completing his academic work, Dr. McKeever was with a consulting firm which specialized in financial investments in petroleum. Those who were following his counsel back in 1954 invested heavily in oil.

For more than ten years he was with IBM, where he held several key management positions. During those years, when IBM was just moving into transistorized computers, he helped that company become what it is today. With IBM, he consulted with top executives of many major corporations in America, helping them solve financial, control and information problems. He has received many awards from IBM, including the "Key Man Award" and the "Outstanding Contribution Award." He is widely known in the computer field for his books and articles on management, management control and information sciences.

In addition to this outstanding business background, Dr. McKeever is an ordained minister. He has been a Baptist evangelist, pastor of Catalina Bible Church for three and a half years (while still with IBM) and a frequent speaker at Christian conferences. He has the gift of teaching and an in-depth knowledge of the Bible, and has authored seven best-selling Christian books, four of which have won the "Angel Award."

Dr. McKeever is president of Omega Ministries, which is a nonprofit organization established under the leading of the Holy Spirit to minister to the body of Christ by the traveling ministry of anointed men of God, through books, cassettes, seminars, conferences, and video tapes. He is the editor of the widely-read newsletter, *End-Times News Digest* (published by Omega Ministries), which relates the significance of current events to biblical prophecy and to the body of Christ today. The worldwide outreach of Omega Ministries is supported by the gifts of those who are interested.

DETAILED OUTLINE

SPECIAL VICTORY PACKAGE
To Help You in the End Times

We have picked three of Dr. McKeever's books that we feel will help you the most in understanding the end times and preparing for them. You can have them at a special discounted price of $14 for *all three!*

The Coming Climax of History — A work that beautifully integrates the prophetic writings of the Old and New Testaments, pulling together many loose ends with startling insights.

You Can Overcome — By far the most important preparation for Christians to make for the difficult days ahead is spiritual preparation. This book helps you understand what it really means to be an overcomer, and how to go about it.

Revelation for Laymen — At last! A clear, readable study of the book of Revelation, geared for plain folks.

☐ Enclosed is $15 for the 3 books described above. BC-915
  (Price subject to change without notice.)

Name:_____

Address_____

City, State:_____Zip:_____

END-TIMES
NEWS
DIGEST

The *End-Times News Digest* is a newsletter published by Omega Ministries. In the main article, Dr. James McKeever shares his latest thinking on prophecy, world events, the economy and Bible topics.

The *End-Times News Digest* not only reports the news that is important to Christians, much of which they may have missed in our controlled media, but also gives an analysis of it from the perspective of a Spirit-filled Christian. In addition, it suggests actions and alternatives that would be appropriate for a Christian to take.

The *End-Times News Digest* also has a regular column on nutrition and health — how to be good stewards of our physical "temple" - as well as items on physical preparation and various aspects of a self-supporting life-style. The spiritual preparation section deals with issues of importance to both the individual Christian and the body of believers.

The contributing writers to this newsletter are Spirit-filled Christians. Dr. James McKeever is the editor and major contributing writer. God gives him insights that will help you, enlighten you, and lift you up spiritually.

This monthly newsletter is sent to anyone who contributes at least $20 per year to Omega Ministries.

Omega Ministries   BC-915
P.O. Box 1788
Medford, OR 97501

☐ Enclosed is a $20 contribution. Please send me *End-Times News Digest* for a year.

☐ Enclosed is $10 for six months.

Name_____

Address_____

City, State_____Zip_____

DEEPER LIFE BOOKLETS
by Dr. James McKeever

HOW YOU CAN KNOW THE WILL OF GOD

One of the most frequent questions asked of Christian leaders by believers is some form of "How can I know the will of God?"

In this excellent booklet, of the Deeper Life series, Dr. McKeever gives a clear and Biblical answer to that.

He first discusses the reasons why God may not be guiding an individual. He then discusses the five ways that God guides a Christian: 1) multitude of counselors, 2) circumstances, 3) the Scriptures, 4) direct revelation, and 5) peace in your heart.

This booklet shows how a Christian can recognize and be tuned into these different ways the that God can guide him.

ONLY ONE WORD

In this booklet the author gives a profound insight into how to establish a deep and exciting relationship with Christ. One pastor said of this booklet, "Everybody in the church should review this booklet constantly. It should be reread until it is memorized and becomes a part of each believer." Hundreds of Christians have written saying that this booklet provided the key for greater fulfillment and happiness in their Christian life.

KNOWLEDGE OF GOOD AND EVIL

In the garden of Eden, God gave His first commandment to man by instructing Adam and Eve not to eat of the Tree of Knowledge of Good and Evil. Does that commandment have any implications for us today? The teaching of this biblically-based booklet is that God still does not want man to have the knowledge of good and evil. The author explains how we can have God guide our decision making rather to "lean" on our own understanding or logic.

WHY WERE YOU CREATED?

The message of this outstanding devotional booklet is that everything in nature does what it was created to do except man. People, even Christians, do not know what the Bible says they were created to do. This produces conflict and purposelessness in the lives of multitudes of Christians. The booklet explains why we were created and tells what we must do to be in tune with God's creative purposes.

(You may write to this publisher for information on these booklets.)

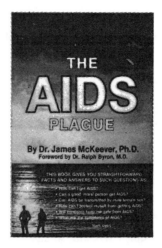

CASSETTES BY DR. JAMES McKEEVER

CASSETTE ALBUMS
Qty Contribution

____$_____*Faith in Action - The Book of James,*
          (6 tapes) $30

____ _____*Become Like Jesus,* (6 tapes) $30

____ _____*The End Times of this Age,*
          (6 tapes) $30

____ _____*Christians Prepare,* (6 tapes) $30

____ _____*You Can Overcome,* (6 tapes) $30

____ _____*The Book of Revelation is Understandable,*
          (16 tapes) $60

SINGLE CASSETTES ($5 each)

____ _____*Judgement Upon America*

____ _____*Eternal Security Vs. Falling From Grace*

____ _____*The Two Keys to Understanding Prophecy*

____ _____*Spend an Hour in Prayer with James McKeever*

____ _____**TOTAL ENCLOSED**

____ _____**Additional Gift for Omega Ministries**

━━━━━━━━━━━━━━━━━━━━━━━━━━━━━━━━━━━━━━

Omega Ministries   BC-915
P.O. Box 1788
Medford, OR 97501

Please ship me the cassettes indicated above
(Prices subject to change without notice.)

Name_____

Address_____

City, State_____Zip_____

FINANCIAL GUIDANCE
By Dr. James McKeever

Here is a book written for Christians explaining in easy-to-understand language how to combine modern profit-making techniques with biblical principles and wisdom, in order to be ready for the chaotic financial conditions ahead. This book is a must for anyone interested in being a good steward over the assets that God has entrusted to him. Being written from a biblical perspective by a noted free-market economist and investment counselor, this book is one of a kind and is filled with valuable information.

The forms in this book will help you analyze your present financial status, factoring in inflation, so as to enable you to intelligently plan and invest.

The chapter titles are as follows:

1. The Foundation is First
2. Three Critical Trends
3. Hurricane Inflation
4. How to Get Money to Invest
5. Developing Your Plan of Action
6. Savings versus Investing
7. Real Estate
8. Gold and Silver
9. Collectibles
10. Stocks and Bonds
11. Commodities
12. Tax Considerations
13. Insurance, Wills and Your Estate
14. The Multinational Individual
15. Prayer, Planning, Prayer, Action
16. Tyranny of the Urgent

This outstanding Christian money management guide helps the reader learn how to assess his present financial condition and specifically how he can invest his savings in ways that will make him a better steward.

(You may use the convenient order form on the last page to order this book.)

SPECIAL VICTORY PACKAGE
To Help You in the End Times

We have picked three of Dr. McKeever's books that we feel will help you the most in understanding the end times and preparing for them. You can have them at a special discounted price of $14 for *all three!*

The Coming Climax of History — A work that beautifully integrates the prophetic writings of the Old and New Testaments, pulling together many loose ends with startling insights.

You Can Overcome — By far the most important preparation for Christians to make for the difficult days ahead is spiritual preparation. This book helps you understand what it really means to be an overcomer, and how to go about it.

Revelation for Laymen — At last! A clear, readable study of the book of Revelation, geared for plain folks.

☐ Enclosed is $15 for the 3 books described above.   BC-915
   (Price subject to change without notice.)

Name:_____

Address_____

City, State:_____Zip:_____

COMMITMENT TO BE A BONDSLAVE AND AN OVERCOMER TO THE GLORY OF GOD THE FATHER, AND HIS SON, JESUS CHRIST

TO THE GOD OF ETERNITY,

I am voluntarily becoming a bondslave of Yours. I have no property nor possessions of my own. I have no time nor rights of my own. I am willing to permanently be Your slave.

I am willing to put on Your armor and to fight against Your enemies. I am willing to do absolutely anything You tell me to do, even if it goes against my knowledge of what is good. I am willing to die for You. Nothing is more important than doing Your will—not my family, my (former) possessions, my job, nor even my own life.

Through Your power I will be an overcomer, not to my glory, but only to Your glory and the glory of Your Son and my Savior, Jesus Christ.

I make this lifetime commitment, not because I have to, nor because of rewards. I make it because of my love for You, because I desire to please You, and because I want to be as close to You as possible throughout eternity.

Signed_____ Date _____

Witness _____ Date _____

JOIN WITH US

If you would like to join with other committed bondslaves to keep in touch and to possibly help each other, send us a copy of this page. We feel that the Lord is raising up an army and we want to be part of His special troops. Perhaps this part of God's army will become known as "The Omega Force." At some point, we may have a conference just for bondslaves that will not be announced to anyone else.

We are going to need each other when persecution starts. Let's help one another to be good soldiers for Jesus Christ.

To: James McKeever, P.O. Box 1788, Medford, Oregon 97501

☐   Yes, I would like to keep in touch with others who have also made a commitment to be a bondslave and an overcomer.

Name _____

Address _____

City, State _____ Zip _____

Home phone ( ) _____ Business phone ( ) _____

Occupation _____

COMMITMENT TO BE A BONDSLAVE AND AN OVERCOMER TO THE GLORY OF GOD THE FATHER, AND HIS SON, JESUS CHRIST

TO THE GOD OF ETERNITY,

I am voluntarily becoming a bondslave of Yours. I have no property nor possessions of my own. I have no time nor rights of my own. I am willing to permanently be Your slave.

I am willing to put on Your armor and to fight against Your enemies. I am willing to do absolutely anything You tell me to do, even if it goes against my knowledge of what is good. I am willing to die for You. Nothing is more important than doing Your will—not my family, my (former) possessions, my job, nor even my own life.

Through Your power I will be an overcomer, not to my glory, but only to Your glory and the glory of Your Son and my Savior, Jesus Christ.

I make this lifetime commitment, not because I have to, nor because of rewards. I make it because of my love for You, because I desire to please You, and because I want to be as close to You as possible throughout eternity.

Signed_____ Date _____

Witness _____ Date _____

JOIN WITH US

If you would like to join with other committed bondslaves to keep in touch and to possibly help each other, send us a copy of this page. We feel that the Lord is raising up an army and we want to be part of His special troops. Perhaps this part of God's army will become known as "The Omega Force." At some point, we may have a conference just for bondslaves that will not be announced to anyone else.

We are going to need each other when persecution starts. Let's help one another to be good soldiers for Jesus Christ.

To: James McKeever, P.O. Box 1788, Medford, Oregon 97501

☐   Yes, I would like to keep in touch with others who have also made a commitment to be a bondslave and an overcomer.

Name _____

Address _____

City, State _____ Zip _____

Home phone ( ) _____ Business phone ( ) _____

Occupation _____

TO THE AUTHOR

Some of the services and materials available from Dr. McKeever are shown in summary on the reverse side. Please indicate your area of interest, remove this page and mail it to Omega Ministries.

Dr. McKeever would appreciate hearing any personal thoughts from you. If you wish to comment, write your remarks below on this reply form.

Comments:

ORDER FORM

Omega Ministries   BC-915
P.O. Box 1788
Medford, OR 97501

☐ Please send me a **FREE** six-month subscription to
the *End-Times News Digest*.

☐ Please send me the following books by Dr. McKeever:
(Prices subject to change without notice)

Qty   Contribution
____$_____*The Coming Climax of History* ($7)
____ _____*You Can Overcome* ($7)
____ _____*Christians Will Go Through the Tribulation—*
                  And How to Prepare For It ($6)
____ _____*Become Like Jesus* ($7)
____ _____*Financial Guidance* ($8)
____ _____*Revelation for Laymen* ($6)
____ _____*The AIDS Plague* (Revised and expanded—$7)

Please send me more information about:

☐ Your speaking at our church or Christian conference
☐ Cassette tapes
☐ Video tapes

Please send the materials I have indicated to:

Name _____

Address _____

City, State _____ Zip _____